THE LAST BITE

A Deadline Cozy Mystery - Book 4

SONIA PARIN

This is a work of fiction. Names, characters, places and incidents are the product of the author's imagination or are used fictitiously. Any resemblance to actual persons, living or dead, organizations, events or locales is entirely coincidental.

ISBN-10: 1539303624

ISBN-13: 978-1539303626

Chapter One

ANOTHER WEDDING INVITATION? The third one this week, Eve thought. And all from the same person. She strode over to the fireplace and crouched down. The thick velum page with its beautiful golden script taunted her as she held it over the flames.

Rise above your circumstances, Eve.

You're better than this.

No, I'm not, she couldn't help thinking, her voice small, like a child's.

"Oh, good. The mail's arrived. I always get the loveliest cards from my fans. So unexpected."

Eve shot to her feet and swung around, making sure to tuck the invitation into the back pocket of her jeans. "All set for a day of writing?" she asked her aunt.

"I'm in reading mode now," Mira said.

Eve had gradually become acquainted with her

aunt's peculiar habit of hiding in her writing cave for days on end, working on her bestselling romance novels, and only emerging when she was satisfied with her day's work. When she didn't write, she read, and in-between she went on cruises.

"Aren't you due for a trip?"

"I've postponed it for another month." Mira looked up from the stack of envelopes. "Any chance of you coming along with me some day?"

Eve shrugged. "Possibly. Maybe. I've never been on a cruise."

"We could go on a culinary cruise. You'd love that."

"Is there such a thing?" When she'd sold her restaurant, she'd thought she had put her cooking days behind her, but she'd since decided to embrace her natural talents and incorporate her management skills by opening up an inn on the island. It had now become her work in progress.

"There are cruises catering to all tastes. I was recently invited to do a reading on a book lovers' cruise. I got all excited at first. Then I realized they wanted me to read the whole book."

"In one go?"

Mira shook her head. "Spread over several days. Now that I think about it, the cruise had organized an author from each genre. I wouldn't mind being read to. I might contact them. See if it's not too late. And it would give me the opportunity of engaging with my readers."

"Coffee?" Eve offered.

"Yes, please. Anyway, there are plenty of activities and pampering on cruises. Or you could always just relax and do absolutely nothing. It would be a nice change for you."

Eve tilted her head in thought. A cruise didn't sound at all bad. Everything would be at her fingertips. She'd never traveled, so it would be a brand new experience for her. If she didn't do it now, she might not get the opportunity for a while. Her inn was in the planning stages, but it already demanded all her attention and would continue to do so. At least, until the business was up and running smoothly. Although, knowing herself as well as she did, she'd probably be reluctant to let go of the reins.

"I see you received another one." Mira tapped Eve's back pocket.

"What are you talking about?"

"The invitation."

Eve sighed. "You never miss a thing."

"I'm a writer. I notice everything. So, who's getting married?"

"No one."

"I see." Mira hummed. "It's someone you don't like."

"I never said that."

"The only person I can think of is Charlotte McLain. Your childhood nemesis."

Eve crouched down to check the oven. Her aunt didn't like her supply of cookies interrupted, so Eve made sure she always had some on hand.

"When you were young, every time you came here for the summer, you looked sullen. It always took you days to realize Charlotte McLain wouldn't be around to shadow your every move and make your life miserable."

"She was persistent and thorough."

"It took me ages to get you to talk about her."

Eve shrugged. "I was trying to avoid falling into her trap. She loved being the center of attention, even when she wasn't around. Talking about her defeated the purpose of being on vacation."

"So, she's getting married and she's sent you three invitations in one week. Doesn't she trust the postal service?"

"She's trying to wear me down."

"I think she's desperate for you to attend."

"That's because she wants to flaunt her fiancé." What other reason could there be? Charlotte McLain had always enjoyed her laps of victory. Her entire life had been driven by them.

"And you're not curious?"

"Not curious enough to travel. She's probably having the wedding in some château or a tropical island. Charlotte never did anything by half measures. Hey..." Eve swung around.

Mira stepped back and held the invitation she'd

snatched from her back pocket out of her reach. "You were wrong." Her aunt's eyebrows curved. "She's getting married right here on the island."

Eve's mouth gaped open. She had to force herself to push the word out, "What?"

Charlotte Look-at-Me McLain... Getting married here? On the island.

"You didn't bother to read it."

"I only got as far as reading her name. That was enough." Enough to resurrect her miserable time at boarding school, being forced to share a room with Charlotte who hadn't gone a day without contriving an evil plot to make Eve suffer.

"You'll have to RSVP."

"Who says?"

"Common courtesy."

"You know I don't abide by rules."

"Yes, and that usually lands you in a heap of trouble." Mira smiled. "She sent you three invitations. At least, they're the ones I saw. There might have been more. She's coming close to begging you to attend."

"She only wants me to go so she can... I don't know. I'm sure she has a motive."

"Sharing her happy moment, perhaps?"

Eve rolled her eyes. "Do I need to remind you what she's like? Oh, look. I have new shoes. I must show Eve," Eve mimicked, "She's been making do with the same pair all year. Oh, my parents are taking me to

Paris. I must tell Eve. She never sees her parents." Eve huffed out a breath. "She somehow manipulated everyone into thinking she was a fairy godmother to me."

"That was Charlotte at fifteen. She's all grown up now," Mira reasoned.

"I doubt she's had a personality transplant. She's more likely to be ten times worse."

"And you're ten times better. Isn't it time you did a bit of flaunting?"

"How did we move from talking about a cruise to you pestering me to go to a wedding?"

"I was only biding my time, waiting to see if you'd mention it. As Jill would say, better out than in. Don't you want to talk about the reasons why she's been sending the invitations? It's been years since you last saw her. Maybe she wants to make amends. You could think of it as a reunion. And for all you know, she might have let herself go."

"That's unlikely. If she has, I'd be the last person she'd want to see."

"Oh, well. Perhaps it's for the best. If you go, someone is bound to end up getting killed."

"Mira! How can you say that?"

Mira's eyebrows drew down. "To tell you the truth, I'm surprised I'm still alive."

"Mira," Eve shrieked and threw her hands up in the air. She'd already been accused of being a death knell.

Several months before, her friend Jill had banned her from using any words associated with killing and death, saying every time those words tripped out of her mouth, someone met their end.

As if that could really happen.

Mira laughed. "I'm probably immune because I'm related to you."

"Stop it. You'll all have me believing it."

"And Jill is immune too so maybe it only affects people you're not close to. Now that I think about it, Charlotte is asking for trouble. You're doing her a favor by not going."

"I have a good mind to go just to prove you wrong. It's nonsense."

"Here's Jill. We'll see what she thinks."

Jill strode in, her dogs, Mischief and Mr. Magoo, trailing behind her.

She looked up and frowned. "Should I go out and come back in again... at some other time?"

Both Mira and Eve started talking at once.

"Eve is afraid of going to a wedding."

"I'm not going and that's final."

Jill held her hands up. "You're squabbling? I'm shocked at you."

Eve folded her arms across her chest. "I'm only saying I reserve the right to turn down an invitation, especially one that guarantees I will have the worst time of my life."

"Mira? Is there something you wish to add?"

"I think Eve is now afraid if she goes someone will end up dead."

Jill tapped her chin. "That's a fair observation. Eve, do you have something to say in your defense?"

"That's enough from you two. I don't like it when you join forces and amuse yourselves at my expense."

"We should call Jack and ask his opinion," Jill suggested.

"Don't you dare. He has nothing to do with this." Although, she couldn't help wondering how he'd feel about accompanying her. Eve turned the oven off and set the tray of cookies on a cooling rack. She'd have to make Jill promise she wouldn't talk about the wedding when Jack was around. They'd been dating for a few months now and Eve was in no hurry to start dropping hints or to have him think she'd started making plans...

"I assume the invitation includes a plus one. That means he does have a say in the matter. Don't you agree, Mira?"

"I do." Mira grinned.

"I'm going to pretend you're not even here."

Mira turned to Jill. "Do you know, she received three invitations and she hasn't answered a single one."

Jill wagged her finger at Eve. "There's never an excuse for rudeness."

"It's refreshing to hear someone as young as you saying that."

"Stop it," Eve demanded.

Jill laughed. "What happened to pretending we're not here?"

Eve turned her attention to sliding the cookies onto the cooling rack. Charlotte McLain had been tenacious enough to track her down to the island. Mira had been right in saying there had been more invitations. The first one had been addressed to her apartment in New York and redirected here. Somehow, she'd found out she was living with her aunt.

"Did either of you happen to notice the date on the invitation?" Eve asked as she bit into a cookie.

"Oh, well, that changes everything," Mira said as she scanned the page, "It's next week. That's cutting it close."

"It's almost like a pity invite," Jill said, "An afterthought."

"An afterthought?" Eve mused. "Yes, I can just imagine Charlotte looking up from her meticulous... pedantic list of things to do for her wedding and realizing she'd forgotten something. Something essential. She would have gone through her list, ticking each item off as she went and then it would have hit her. Oh, yes. The entertainment. I can't believe I've been so remiss, she would have said. Must invite Eve Lloyd." She held up the platter of cookies. "Would anyone like a cookie?"

"Mm... smells good," Jill helped herself to one.

"Cinnamon?" Mira asked.

"With honey and hazelnuts." Eve wiped the counter and emptied the dishwasher. "Mira, do you mind if Mischief and Mr. Magoo stay here with you? Jill wanted to get some art supplies and I'm running low on chocolate." She'd also been compiling a long list of must have items for her new inn. Nothing she needed to get straightaway. At the moment, she was open to inspiration.

"So long as they're happy to sit by the fireplace. I intend spending my morning reading."

"They've had their long walk," Jill said and snatched a couple of cookies for the drive into town.

"Okay, I'm ready." Eve grabbed a leather jacket she hadn't worn in ages. The weather continued to cool down, which again made her wonder why Charlotte would pick this location for her nuptials. Shouldn't she want somewhere warmer? Oh, how Eve wished Charlotte would change her mind. It wouldn't take much effort. Charlotte could manage it at the blink of an eye. She'd always been a whirlpool of activity, organizing her social life, manipulating her friends into doing her bidding, trespassing on Eve's peace of mind, always managing to find her, no matter where she hid...

"Are you taking the long way to town?" Jill asked as Eve drove off in the opposite direction.

"Something's off about all this. Why would Charlotte McLain choose such an out of the way place for the most significant event of her life? I have to see the venue." She handed Jill the invitation. "Look the address up for me, please."

"You mean, the scene of the next crime?"

"Please don't joke about it. I think we've had enough murder and mayhem to last us a lifetime. The odds of this shindig being uneventful are stacked in her favor. She's in luck."

"This is the Stevenson house. Rumor has it, they're cash poor at the moment. Jason Stevenson has been having a run of bad luck with his investments and his wife has run through all the money she inherited, or so she says. It makes sense to hire out the house. You can't miss it. It's the largest on the island."

"What do you mean, or so she says?"

"She comes from old money. The type that doesn't run out. She's probably stashed it away in some off-shore account, well out of her husband's greedy reach."

Eve frowned. "I don't know who you are. Where's this cynicism coming from?"

"I think I've been hanging around you for too long." Jill looked up and pointed ahead. "Follow those catering trucks. They're bound to be heading there."

"How do you know they're catering trucks?"

"You're kidding. It's right there in front of you. Mayflower Catering written in stylish script."

"I was watching the road."

Within minutes, the house... or rather, the estate

came into view and then disappeared behind a copse of tall firs.

Eve bit her bottom lip. The house could be as grand as Buckingham Palace, it still didn't make sense. A wedding at The Ritz London... Paris... anywhere but here, that was more Charlotte's style. "Maybe the groom hails from around here."

"The name doesn't ring a bell."

"Then there could be a connection with the Stevenson family. If you say she comes from old money, that's something she has in common with Charlotte." Or maybe, Mira was right and Charlotte had changed. Charlotte... or her circumstances.

Chapter Two

"THE ENTOURAGE IS ARRIVING."

Eve looked up from the magazine she'd been flicking through and gazed around the Chin Wag Café.

Despite her efforts to ignore the rising murmurs around her, she'd spent the last half hour listening to an on-going commentary of the cars driving along the main street, presumably on their way to the Stevenson house. Charlotte McLain hadn't even arrived and, surprise, surprise... not, she'd already become the talk of the town.

Eve drew out a chair for Jill. "Sit down, I'm famished."

"You should have gone ahead and ordered."

"Mira's been on my case about not sending the RSVP. I'm trying to show I'm not a complete philistine. I do have some manners. And why are you so late?"

"I stopped to chat with Steffi Grant and Linda Brennan. They've been counting the cars driving into the Stevenson house. Thirty-five at the last count. One glitzier than the other."

"What do you think of this table setting for my inn?" Eve asked, "I'm trying to keep the country charm Abby had going." She still couldn't quite believe she'd gone ahead and purchased Abby Larkin's beach house. The memory of the dead body she'd found there had only now began to recede, but not entirely. Right on cue, Eve shivered.

"Sorry, did you say something?" Jill asked.

"I tried to steer the conversation away from my nemesis—"

"Sh."

"What?"

"Haven't you learned anything? After all that's happened, you should know better than to voice your grievances out loud and in a public place. Now everyone within hearing knows there's bad blood between you and the bride."

"The bride? How are they going to know my nemesis is Charlotte McLain?"

Jill spread her arms out. "You just told them."

Eve drew in a sharp breath. "From now on, I'll start my day with a caveat. Anything I say can and will be held against me in a court of law. How's that?"

"It's a practical, sensible step. I can't always be there to act as your alibi."

Frowning, she leaned forward and lowered her voice. "You do realize those were unusual circumstances." Three deaths since her arrival on the island. And before that...

Nothing.

Not a single incident had ever been recorded. Not even a fishing boat accident, and the island had a long history of attracting weekend fishing enthusiasts.

Eve had decided to put it down as an unnatural short-term imbalance that would no doubt rectify itself with endless days of perfect tedium.

"You can pretend life has returned to normal, but I prefer to be on guard," Jill murmured, "By the way, have you noticed that woman staring at you?"

"I refuse to play your game." Eve returned her attention to her magazine and the article she'd been reading about small town inns.

"She doesn't look like a local. In fact, I'm willing to bet she's with the wedding party."

"I should start attending estate sales and see what I can pick up there," Eve said, "Abby's house came fully furnished, but I'll need more small tables and chairs for the new dining area. They'll have to be antiques, of course."

"She's still looking at you in that sort of where-do-I-know-her-from way."

Eve tapped the page she was reading. “I could work my way up the coast. Spend an entire weekend hopping from one estate sale to the other.”

Jill chuckled. “Just think of it, all those people dying to leave you their stuff. And, by the way, she’s still looking. Now she’s pulling out her cell phone. I’m guessing she’s going to call you to see if you are who she thinks you are.”

Eve forced her gaze to remain on the magazine. She gritted her teeth. She growled under her breath. Her hand inched toward her cell phone.

It rang.

Don’t answer it!

“She’ll leave a message. In your place, I’d get it over and done with right now.”

Eve sighed and answered the call, the feeling of having picked up the gauntlet making her body quiver with a wave of anxiety. “Yes, hello.”

“Eve Lloyd? From Northlands Academy?”

You called me, you should know...

“Um, yes.”

“It’s Charlotte.”

“Charlotte?”

“Charlotte McLain.”

The enemy had been engaged. No turning back now.

She lifted her chin slightly. “Charlotte. I’ve been trying to contact you.”

“You have?”

"Yes. I believe congratulations are in order. I received your wedding invitations but they all came with no return address." An outright lie. The best she could come up with on the spur of the moment. Eve hoped her cheeks hadn't given her away with a deep flush of crimson red. She kept her gaze fixed on the magazine article, pretending Charlotte's call hadn't raised her heart rate or dried her mouth.

"I'll have to have a word with my assistant."

Eve looked out the window.

Charlotte stood on the sidewalk staring right at her, a smug smile in place. In an instant, she replaced it with her version of friendliness, her perfect lips forming a small o of surprise. She raised her hand and gave her a small, royal wave.

Eve's stomach tightened. In less than a second, Eve had managed to get Charlotte's assistant fired. Charlotte would make sure to follow through on the unspoken threat.

"Serendipity," Charlotte said. "Don't move, I'm coming in." She slipped her cell phone inside her luxurious handbag, targeted a stray lock, set it in place, and made a beeline toward the café. Charlotte McLain had launched her take-no-prisoners offensive attack.

"I'm afraid I might have set something in motion," she told Jill.

"And now it's too late to back out?"

Eve nodded. "I've been pushed through the rabbit hole."

Jill clicked her fingers in front of Eve's unblinking eyes. "Eve. Are you still with us?"

She shook her head. "Too late now."

"There you are," Charlotte said in her familiar breezy tone that had now acquired a firm edge. "All these years and you haven't changed a single thing about yourself. The same old Eve Lloyd. It's almost comforting, like an old pair of shoes you keep in the closet because you can't bear to part with them."

The air kissing was new. But the rest...

Vintage Charlotte.

Eve introduced Jill, who sat back, her mouth gaping open either in awe or shock. Eve couldn't decide. She only knew Charlotte had already secured her acquiescence. Her assistant's livelihood depended on Eve doing as told... or else.

She wondered if she had something suitable to wear. Then again, it didn't matter what she wore. Charlotte would find a way to make her feel inadequate.

Remember, Eve, you alone decide how you feel.

Eve gave a small, firm nod. No one had the power to reign over her.

She tried to hold onto the thought, to recite it like a mantra, but then she saw Jill's expression shift from awe to appreciation.

What had she missed?

"An artist," Charlotte was saying, "Well, that is fantastic. Where do you show your paintings?"

No, Jill... No, don't look into her eyes.

"I always have a few displayed at The Mad Hatter's Teashop across the road."

"A teashop? Your work should be hanging in an art gallery. Eve, why haven't you done something to help your friend?"

That's right, it was her fault.

She'd failed to guide Jill onto the right path.

"All my friends collect art," Charlotte went on to say, "I'm sure they'll be delighted to acquire one of your pictures. We'll come visit your studio..."

In the blink of an eye, she'd lost her friend to the dark side. Now it would be up to her to launch a rescue. Eve hoped it didn't turn into a mercy mission where she'd only find scattered bits and pieces of Jill Saunders as she'd known her.

Charlotte turned to her. "Since my assistant failed to provide you with the return address envelope, we'll consider this your RSVP. Save you the trouble."

Charlotte gave her a winning smile which Eve returned, never mind that her back teeth were gritting.

"I've planned an entire week of events starting with tonight's cocktail party. I'll see you there at eight."

With her mission accomplished, Charlotte rose and left, the scent of victory trailing behind her.

"Are you all right?" she asked Jill.

Jill blinked.

Eve sighed. "She has that effect on us lesser beings." While she included herself, Eve wanted to believe she'd grown a thicker skin. In all the years she'd known Charlotte, Eve had tried to uncover the secret to her success as a master manipulator. The universe always yielded to her every demand. Without question, which only went to show how impartial the universe could be.

"I'm in awe of her voice."

"Elocution lessons."

"What?"

"After boarding school," something Eve still couldn't forgive her parents for, "Charlotte attended one of the most prestigious finishing schools in Europe. She'd always been a big fan of 1940s black and white movies, the ones set in high society with heroines wearing flashy diamonds and being chauffeured around the place. She wanted to sound like them." Eve tilted her head in thought. "I wouldn't be surprised if she's since hired someone to write conversation scripts for her. Monday, lunch with Princess so and so from some minor European royal house, talk about her porcelain figurine collection, her personal stylist's lack of taste," Eve shrugged. "It all goes with the territory. I'm afraid our little existence has been overshadowed by her magnificence."

"I'm tempted to say you exaggerate."

That's because Charlotte already had Jill eating out of her hands. "Don't worry, it'll wear off eventually."

"What?"

"Never mind." Becoming conscious of her posture, she sat up straighter.

"She looks... I can't put my finger on it."

"Bigger than life?" Eve suggested.

"Yes. Makes me wonder what her life is like."

"You catch snippets of it on TV. She is one of those incredibly rich people who do nothing but travel, shop and lunch among many other expensive activities. They live by the motto that goes something like 'if it's not expensive, it's not worth doing or having'. We're talking serious money."

"I don't understand why you don't like her."

Eve gazed at her friend and envied her innocence. "Don't ever change, Jill." If given the choice, Eve would prefer to always look on the bright side and see the best in people. But sometimes... they made it so difficult.

"What was the groom's name? I want to see if there's something online about him."

There'd have to be. Charlotte wouldn't dream of marrying a nobody. Eve fished around for the name. "Jon O'Brian." A fairly ordinary sounding name.

"Here's an announcement." Jill sat forward, her cell phone in hand.

"You look disappointed."

"I guess I expected to be dazzled. He looks stocky."

Eve frowned. "Impossible. Let me see. The camera lens doesn't always capture the most flattering aspects." She gazed at the photo. "Maybe it's the angle." He did look stocky. In fact, he looked shorter than Charlotte. "Perhaps they were standing on an incline."

"The article doesn't say anything about him. It's all about the bride."

"That doesn't surprise me." Maybe a little. The Charlotte she knew would want to sing her fiancé's praises. Let the whole world know what an excellent catch he was and how her life was so much brighter than anyone else's.

"Do you think there's any chance of getting an invitation to the wedding?"

Eve counted to ten. She could think of a thousand reasons to spare her friend the experience, but she couldn't say no to the light of hope shining in Jill's eyes. "You could come as my plus one."

Jill clapped her hands. "Could I? Will Jack mind?"

"I'm sure he'll be only too pleased to learn I haven't forced him into wearing a suit and making small talk." She drew in a deep breath but the lump in her stomach didn't budge. "I guess I have to go home and select a little black dress to wear tonight."

Chapter Three

EVE KNEW she could have saved herself a whole lot of trouble by putting on her drabbest dress, but her self-esteem had demanded she put her best foot forward.

Dressed in a low cut sleeveless black cocktail dress, which had only ever seen the light of day... or rather twilight, once, her sling backs and a tiny evening purse unsuitable for anything more than a tube of lipstick, she sashayed into what was probably referred to as a reception room, or maybe even a ballroom.

Eve guessed the Stevenson house had been built during a time when people attended balls. Over two hundred years old, perhaps older, it had been in the Stevenson family since the first stone had been laid. According to Jill, everyone referred to the Stevensons as the first family on the island.

A jazz band played in the background but only a few couples had taken to the dance floor. Everyone else flitted from one group to another, their expensive fragrances mingling as they chatted, ate, drunk and compared massive bank accounts.

A tray hovered near Eve, the waiter keeping himself at arm's length. Eve imagined Charlotte issuing strict instructions to the waiting staff telling them to be inconspicuous because they were there to serve and not to be seen.

She made eye contact with the waiter and smiled. "Thank you." She helped herself to a glass of champagne she recognized as being ridiculously expensive French bubbles.

Eve took a tiny slurp and immediately looked around to see if Charlotte had heard her. No time like the present to incite her wrath and she'd prefer to be deliberate about it and not be caught unawares.

At a glance she knew straight away she had nothing in common with the guests so she prepared herself for an evening of fading into the background.

She wished she could be curled up in her aunt's sitting room, watching the flames dancing in the fireplace, reading a book or working her way through the stack of magazines she had acquired since deciding to set up an inn. Jill had planned on spending the evening painting and Mira had said nothing would take her away from her current book. Still, even if she'd been alone, it would have been better than this.

"You're a new face."

"Do I win a prize?" She looked up, her smile in place as she nodded at the man wearing a slick, made to measure tuxedo. She tried to determine which set he belonged to. Professional idler? Highflier? Eve decided to be nicer. Polo player. Lawyer.

Come on, Eve. You can do better than that.

Surgeon. No, too young.

"I'm Winthorpe."

"Is that a first or a last name?" she asked.

"Both."

"Winthorpe Winthorpe?"

"No, just Winthorpe."

"How unusual."

"Mother."

"Your mother's doing?"

He nodded. "Wanted me to make my mark in the world. Her idea of a head start."

"Has it worked for you?"

"To a point. No one struggles to remember both a first name and a family name." He gave a rich chuckle and downed his glass of, she guessed, the finest Scotch whisky money could provide.

"Bride or groom?" he asked.

Which side? She had to assume that's what he

meant. She also guessed he enjoyed delivering parsimonious sentences, leaving the listener to fill in the gaps.

"Bride." By default, blackmail and a twisted arm.

He gave a small knowing nod. "Me too."

"Would you mind pointing the groom out to me, please?"

He responded with a slight lift of his chestnut colored eyebrow and a tilt toward the general direction of a massive fireplace.

"Next to the shade of aqua."

By that, she supposed, he meant the man standing next to the woman wearing a flowing shift dress in aqua blue.

Eve studied the man Winthorpe had pointed out. She couldn't believe it. The photo hadn't lied. Not very tall and going by the slight tilt of his legs, she guessed he wore lifts and had the habit of bouncing on his feet to give the illusion of an extra half inch or so. Would he even reach Charlotte's shoulders?

"And what does he do?" it seemed safe to ask.

Winthorpe gestured with his glass. "Builds."

Architect? Engineer? Builder?

Bricklayer...

"Has he built anything I might have seen?"

"Been to Asia?"

"Can't say that I have."

"Growing economies."

She gave a knowing nod, although she knew nothing about growing economies in Asia.

"Ah, Eve Lloyd. How lovely to see you after all these years."

Eve turned to Charlotte who'd clearly decided to start with a clean slate. Then again, she'd always excelled at the game of pretense.

She wore a stunning beaded gown the color of smoked salmon. Eve sent her gaze skating around the ballroom and realized more than half the guest wore that shade of smoked salmon, including the men, the color splashed on their ties or handkerchiefs neatly tucked into their pockets.

"I wouldn't have missed it for the world."

Eve received a small smile of approval, Charlotte's version of a pat on the head. Eve supposed that meant she now had to behave. At least for the sake of Charlotte's assistant who would no doubt get the boot for some other contrived misdemeanor. Eve's stomach twisted into a knot. Belatedly, she wished she hadn't lied about the wedding invitations missing a return envelope...

"Come and meet some people."

Eve excused herself and wondered if Winthorpe didn't count as people.

Charlotte guided her toward the opposite end of the room. "That's a lovely dress you're wearing. I'm trying to remember where I saw it. Milan? Paris? No... Wait...

It can't have been as recent as that. I'm thinking... Maybe two years ago, or was it three? Yes, it was on sale at Bergdorf Goodman's. It had been on a quick sale rack and I wondered who'd be desperate enough to buy it. Such a lovely find, I thought. Of course, I could never wear it. I wouldn't be able to face the criticism. You know how some people are..."

Eve smiled. Charlotte hadn't lost her touch, giving with one hand and snatching away with the other.

The introductions came hard and fast. Eve tried to keep up, repeating names in her head and trying to remember the trick of associating them with something she noticed about the person, but even that failed to help her as Charlotte whizzed her from one group to another. Also, it didn't help to hear so many hyphenated names.

"Eve Lloyd. Simple enough to remember," Elizabeth-May Ainsworth-Wright said as if reading her mind.

Had the second part of the name been June she might have linked it to the British queen's birthday, which according to the history lessons that had been drummed into her, was officially in June, while the real birthday was in April. Then it hit her. She could try thinking of the month between April and June.

It didn't help to be introduced to another Elizabeth. This time, Elizabeth-Anne Margaret Grainger. Charlotte was being gracious to add a conversation starter. Elizabeth-Anne Margaret Grainger traveled. Elizabeth-May Ainsworth-Wright also traveled. As did everyone else it seemed. Including the men. Did no one work for a living these days?

Remembering the men's names became as much of a trial for Eve. They all came with numbers at the end. Elton Mortimer III. Joshua Gill Maguire IV. Eve began to miss Winthorpe...

As they inched their way toward the groom, the guests Charlotte introduced her to appeared to lose prestige, dropping the hyphens and numbers, but not their wealth, Eve thought.

Any minute now she'd be introduced to the man himself. Saving the best till last?

Eve smiled and nodded until her head ached and a trickle of perspiration ran down her back.

Could she leave now?

What if she came down with... a bout of spinelessness? Charlotte couldn't expect her to be the life of the party if she didn't have a spine to hold her upright.

Why not just leave, Eve?

No one would notice her absence.

Yeah, right.

No one except Charlotte.

Picking up what could only be described as a disturbance in the universe, Eve glanced at Charlotte. Someone had approached her. A woman in a gray suit. Stylish yet demure. Her assistant?

Eve tried to listen to the whispered exchange but the group around her burst into laughter so the words were drowned out. Clearly something had happened. The edge of Charlotte's lip twitched.

Charlotte turned to her. "This is a disaster."

"I haven't tried the *hors d'oeuvres* yet, but the champagne is... exquisite," Eve said and took a sip of her drink, this time making sure she didn't slurp. Charlotte looked about ready to explode. Her lips had tightened. The veins on her temples bulged. In her mind, Eve took a step away and followed it with a hasty retreat. She'd witnessed one of Charlotte's explosions once when something hadn't gone her way...

"The sushi chef has taken ill."

"Get one of the others to cover for him." It sounded like a simple enough solution to Eve. It's what she would have done in any situation. Share the burden and responsibility. That's what teamwork was all about.

Charlotte's eyes nearly bulged out. Of all the ridiculous suggestions, that would have to be the worst one, she could almost hear Charlotte say.

"I'll be the laughing stock. Eve, you're a chef. What do you suggest I do?"

She'd only had two sips of her champagne. Not enough to impair her memory. Hadn't she just made a suggestion? A practical one? One any sensible person would agree with?

"Take the sushi off the menu?"

Charlotte's mouth gaped open. "That's the best you can come up with?"

As a guest? Yes. As a reluctant guest, Charlotte was lucky to get anything out of her. Eve's glance shifted to the woman in the gray suit. She looked grim. Her hand shot to her stomach. Her lips quivered. She gave the slightest shake of her head, as if pleading with Eve to please not make the problem worse than it already was.

"The guests have already seen the itinerary, including the menu. Tonight, they were expecting sushi." Charlotte swung toward her assistant. "And they will get sushi."

The assistant took a hard swallow.

"Perhaps..." Don't do it, Eve. She cleared her throat. "Perhaps I could see if I—"

"Would you?" Charlotte asked.

"Ms. McLain insists all chefs wear this."

Eve looked at the pristine white chef's outfit and clogs and warmed at its familiarity. "Where can I change?"

The assistant pointed her in the direction of the powder room next to the massive kitchen.

"What's your name?" Eve asked.

"Marjorie."

"I'm Eve."

Marjorie nodded. "Are... are you sure you can do this? Ms. McLain has expectations..."

High expectations. Impossible benchmarks. Ludicrous standards. Eve knew only too well.

"Don't worry. I'm trained." In everything but Sushi making. But how hard could it be?

Shortly after changing out of her cocktail dress and into the more comfortable pants and jacket, she returned, her eyes admiring the large cooker taking pride of place in the middle of the spacious kitchen.

"Are you acquainted with the oven?"

"*La Cornue Château* Series," Eve murmured. She continued to admire the custom made French oven and cooking range. She had considered getting one for the inn... a much smaller version, of course, and had been dazzled by the service provided when she'd made inquiries. These little beauties were handcrafted and if she went ahead with her order, she would be assigned a project manager who would oversee the entire production process from start to finish. There hadn't been any mention of cost, but Eve imagined anyone needing to ask wouldn't be able to afford it. So, she'd added it to her wish list, the one she'd put away in a bottom drawer...

"Right... well." She looked around her. There were five chefs at work, and several kitchen hands, all assigned their workstations and treating them like prime real estate.

"Some of the ingredients have already been prepared."

Eve went to stand in her allotted space.

Marjorie handed her a piece of paper. "These are the instructions for Mr. Jon O'Brian's sushi. He doesn't eat fish."

Eve scanned the page.

Duck sushi.

"How soon do you think you can have them out?"

As soon as she could access the Internet to figure out how to make sushi to perfection...

Eve looked over her shoulder. One of the kitchen hands glanced at her and quickly looked away. She was on her own...

"They were scheduled to be in circulation in half an hour."

"I'll see what I can do."

Marjorie gave her a pleading look.

"Yes. Half an hour."

Eve allocated five minutes to doing a crash course on sushi preparation.

Apparently, Jon O'Brian had hunted these ducks himself and he liked nothing better than to eat what he killed.

Each to his own, Eve thought and worked out a way to produce enough to go out within minutes. Humming to herself, she focused on efficiently keeping the production line moving.

She sensed the other chefs giving her furtive glances. When she made eye contact with them she couldn't help feeling they looked wary. Actually, Eve thought they looked scared.

"So... what happened to the other chef?" she asked in an effort to break the ice.

She heard a few low grumbles and a muttered reply. Nothing she could actually make out.

The waiters appeared and took away three platters of perfectly formed sushi.

When another waiter appeared, Eve said, "This is the special platter for Jon O'Brian."

Along with the duck, she'd also had to spread the nori sheet with a thin layer of duck liver *pâté*. As per strict instructions.

Really... the sushi Gods had to be rolling their eyes at her.

She finished just as her fingers began to cramp.

The repetitive action guaranteed she'd be rolling sushi in her sleep.

After cleaning up, Eve changed out of her chef's outfit and into her own clothes and considered making a swift getaway. No one would notice her absence. No one would care.

Take your leave of the hostess...

She mentally swatted the prissy little voice in her head.

She would do no such thing.

Yet she made her way back to the ballroom. With

any luck, she might be able to catch Charlotte deep in conversation and wave to her from a distance.

The shriek, blood curdling and, surely loud enough to shatter a crystal glass, broke her stride.

Eve steadied herself, one hand pressing against her chest, the other leaning against the wall.

Had Charlotte found a hair in the sushi?

Chapter Four

EVE KNEW THE DRILL. Even if a part of her hollered to run for her life, she had to take forward steps and face the music.

Worse case scenario? Charlotte would humiliate her in public. Eve didn't care. None of these people meant anything to her. After tonight, she'd never see them again.

Gathering her confidence, she hurried toward the ballroom in time to see everyone moving toward a central point in the room, leaning down and then shuffling back. It almost looked like a scene out of a ballet or one of those nature documentaries where pink feathered flamingos performed a ritual dance, all moving in unison...

A gasp rose and fell.

As the way cleared, Eve's gaze fell on the man lying

prostrate on the floor, Charlotte kneeling beside him, her arms outstretched.

Another image formed in her mind.

A scene straight out of a tragic opera.

Staged, she thought and then realized that was Jon O'Brian lying on the floor.

"What's going on?" she asked even as instinct kicked in and she dug inside her minuscule evening bag for her cell phone. "Has someone called an ambulance?"

No one replied, but the sound of her voice was taken as a prompt to empty glasses in single gulps.

She knew the feeling.

"Does he have a pulse? Is there a doctor here?" she asked still moving toward Jon O'Brian.

Again, no one spoke.

Seeing her approaching, Charlotte waved her hand as if dismissing her. Little did she know Eve was the one and only person here she wanted nearby. The only person, it seemed, with any practical skills. She wouldn't necessarily call herself an expert, but her credentials had grown exponentially with her recently acquired firsthand experience.

"Yes," she answered the operator's businesslike greeting.

State your emergency.

How could she classify this? Man about to draw his last breath? She watched to see if his chest rose. For long seconds it didn't move. Finally, it collapsed and Jon O'Brian's head rolled to the side.

"Ambulance," she managed. "Pulse?" She felt for one and couldn't detect it. "Hurry." CPR, she thought but before she could place her hands on his chest, someone grabbed her by the waist and hauled her away. Her gaze landed on Charlotte's eyes, wide and filled with what could only be described as accusation, her finger pointed straight at Eve.

"You," she said.

Then it all became clear.

Next to Jon O'Brian lay the platter of sushi.

Duck sushi.

Eve sat in a corner of the vast kitchen. Everyone else sat or stood on the opposite side, staring at her.

Glancing toward the window, she caught the reflection of an ambulance leaving.

Had they arrived in time to save him?

She didn't hear the sirens blaring so she guessed the answer would be no.

She sensed everyone straightening.

Eve slid to the edge of her chair.

Jack.

He stood by the doorway, his gaze skating around

the kitchen. When Detective Mason Lars appeared, Eve knew the ambulance had taken away a body.

"Who prepared the sushi?" Jack asked, his voice instantly drawing everyone's attention.

Several fingers shot out and pointed at Eve.

One person spoke up, "She did."

Eve's head lowered slightly and she sunk into her chair.

Jack exchanged a few words with Mason Lars. She'd seen that happen often enough to know what came next. Jack wouldn't excuse himself from the case, but he'd step back and hand the reins over to Detective Mason Lars.

To her surprise, Jack approached her, his gaze steady on her and impossible to read.

"Let's go."

"Where?"

He didn't answer.

A glance at the kitchen staff made her grateful they would all be excused from jury duty. In their eyes, the guilt lay entirely... solely at her feet.

Jack escorted her out of the house. Guests hovered in the wide entranceway. Eyes were cast her way. Whispers exchanged. Verdicts predicted. A lynch mob in the making, Eve thought.

When they reached the squad car, Jack placed his hand on her head to prevent her hitting it as she eased into the back seat.

He rounded the car and got in beside her. A police officer took the driver's seat.

"What's going on, Jack? I drove myself here. My car's back there."

"I couldn't very well let you drive yourself home."

"Why not?"

He pushed out a weary breath. "How do you know Charlotte McLain?"

"I... I went to school with her, but don't hold that against me."

"So, you two are not the best of friends."

"I'd have to be hallucinating to make that claim."

"So, what were you doing at her cocktail party?"

"She insisted I come."

"You're not friends, but you felt compelled to attend."

She gestured with her hands. "If you knew Charlotte you'd understand she has ways of making people do her bidding, march to the beat of her tune, kowtow to her."

The officer driving flicked his gaze her way. Had she said too much?

"When was the last time you saw each other?"

She wanted to say over twenty years before when they'd been at boarding school together, but there had been that one time when Charlotte had come into her restaurant.

"I didn't keep in touch. But she has ways of keeping track of me."

"Sounds like you two have a shared history."

Something caught in her throat. A laugh. A breath. She couldn't be sure. "Am I being officially questioned?"

"Not yet."

When she saw the officer take a turn into Mira's street, Eve's breath relaxed.

"We'll take a statement from you in the morning."

"What about the others? The guests? You're not letting them go."

"Did you notice anyone acting suspiciously?"

"I'll have to think about that. In all honestly, I didn't spend that much time with them. Charlotte had me whisked off to the kitchen."

"I thought you were a guest."

"I was, until the sushi chef fell ill. You might want to find out what happened to him. In fact, I would make that a priority." She dug her fingers through her hair. "What about my car?"

"Give me the keys. I'll drive it back later on."

"There were so many people, Jack. The waiting staff. The chefs. The kitchen hands. The guests. The owners of the house..."

"We'll talk about it tomorrow. Get some rest, Eve."

By the sounds of it, she'd need it.

Eve stood on the front veranda and tried to make sense of the last hour or so.

Jon O'Brian killed.

Why did she assume he'd been killed?

Why not wonder if he'd had a bad response... an allergic reaction... a heart attack that had been a long time coming?

Eve cursed her habit of getting up early. Why couldn't she be like normal people and sleep in until midday? At least once a week...

"You came in late last night, I didn't hear you," Mira said as she strode into the kitchen. At the sight of several plates full of muffins and cookies, Mira looked up at her. "How was the cocktail party?"

"I'd rather not talk about it." She heard Mira's intake of breath. Eve stilled and she suddenly understood the concept of a deer caught in headlights. She held her breath.

"Something happened."

Eve pushed out the breath she'd been holding and took out another tray from the oven.

"Eve?"

She gave an impatient shrug. "All right. I suppose you'll find out sooner or later. The groom is dead."

She turned slightly and saw her aunt's mouth gape open in surprise.

"I know I joked about it... But... When? How?"

"Last night," Eve said trying to sound casual. "By my hands apparently."

"Eve."

She shook her head. "I shouldn't jump to conclusions. For all I know, he might have had a condition, a heart murmur, or some other fatal trigger just waiting to go off. Just my luck to be there when it all happened."

"Why do you think you had something to do with it?"

Eve poured them each a mug of coffee and guided Mira to the table where she filled her in on the events of the night before.

"You were very accommodating helping out when you did."

"Charlotte left me no choice, I had to step in and help out in the kitchen. That sort of put me right in the thick of it." She sighed. "You don't know what she's like when she doesn't get her way. Everything has to be perfect. The slightest hiccup can send her into a tailspin and heaven help anyone around her. Anyhow, I thought I would diffuse the situation but it seems I made it worse."

"By killing her fiancé." Mira gave a small nod of understanding.

Eve frowned.

"Sorry, that just slipped out. Force of habit."

"That's okay. I suppose it doesn't help when I say I made it worse." She brushed her hands across her face.

"I promised Jill yesterday I wouldn't say anything that could be held against me."

"That's very sensible... considering your history."

Eve sprung to her feet. "They're coming for me this morning. The police will want to know everything and I'm afraid I have nothing to say."

"Well then, you tell them that. You can't be held accountable for every death on the island... I mean for someone else's actions."

Someone else.

The killer. He... she had to be in that house.

Eve knew, with absolute certainty, she'd had nothing to do with Jon O'Brian's death. Not directly. Not deliberately. She also suspected there had been nothing natural about the cause of death. "Argh!"

"Perhaps you should drink something more soothing than coffee."

"I need my wits about me, Mira. Jack said he and Detective Mason Lars were coming around this morning to take a statement from me."

"You simply tell them what you know."

"But what if that's not enough? A man is dead and it looks like the food I prepared had something to do with it."

"You shouldn't jump to conclusions. They'll run tests and that could take some time. Besides, you weren't the only one in the kitchen. There were others.

And the house is full of guests. How many did you say she'd invited?"

Eve gestured with her hand. "Possibly over fifty, with more coming for the wedding. Or at least I assume there will be... would have been." She strode around the kitchen. "There's been something odd from the start. The fact she's even having... or had planned on having the wedding here sounded off to me. If I ever stopped to think about it, I'd imagine Charlotte's wedding would be a highlight in the social calendar with hundreds of people attending. Having it here, in this out of the way place..." she spread her hands out, "The Stevenson house is large, but I doubt it can accommodate more than a dozen couples. She'd planned a week's worth of partying before the actual wedding."

"I think that's someone at the door," Mira said.

Eve drew in a deep breath. "It has to be Jack." She strode along the hallway, her brows drawn down in frustration. As a chef, she'd been trained to work in the midst of chaos without losing her focus on the task at hand. It was all part and parcel of working in a busy kitchen, dealing with people while trying to prepare meals. That was the easy part; the order and the process of making things, of cooking and baking. Follow a recipe to the letter and you were rewarded with perfect results. In her world, everyone and everything had a purpose.

But this... this unknown chaos with hidden motives remained beyond her understanding. It frustrated her.

Lost in her thoughts, she opened the door. It wasn't Jack.

"Charlotte."

She wore head to toe black, her rich chocolate brown locks cascading from underneath a beret. Large sunglasses hid her eyes, but Eve didn't need to see them to know they were hard and filled with fury. She could see it in her lips, pressed tightly together.

"Come in."

Charlotte gave a brisk shake of her head. "I only came here to ask why, why did you do it? Do you hate me that much?"

If Eve hadn't been holding the doorknob, she would have stumbled back. Charlotte honestly thought Eve had killed her fiancé.

"You're in shock." It was the only comment she could think of. To her ears, her remark sounded insensitive, callous. Inconsiderate. She tried to put herself in Charlotte's place. Would she lash out and point the finger of blame at the most obvious target? Or would she move heaven and earth to find the person responsible?

"The police are doing everything in their power to find the..." The killer? She assumed there'd be an autopsy performed and until then...

"Go ahead, say it."

"We won't know for sure until it's made official."

"I've heard about you and the detective. Very convenient, Eve."

Eve pressed her lips together. Arguing wouldn't serve any purpose. Charlotte needed to vent her frustration and navigate her way through the grieving process.

Eve tried to remember the five steps of grieving.

Charlotte would have spent little time with denial. Jon O'Brian was dead and once the body had been removed, there'd be no coming back from that. As for isolation...

She might have locked herself up in her room for the night, but it had been brief.

This had to be the anger stage, Eve thought. Then again, Charlotte had started with that step the night before.

"Would you like to come in?"

Charlotte swayed slightly and then took a step back. Her hands clutched the straps of her handbag.

"You will pay for this. If not through the legal system, then... You will pay." She swung away and stormed down the path.

Eve stood at the door, the bitter aftertaste of the encounter lingering in her mouth.

Then she remembered the next step in the grieving process.

Bargaining.

She wouldn't put it past Charlotte to bargain with the devil himself to get her justice.

She was about to close the front door when she saw Jack drive in. He hadn't come alone. This would be an official visit.

Eve stepped back and let them through gesturing to the front sitting room.

"How about some coffee, Eve," Jack said and instead moved toward the kitchen.

Mira greeted the detectives and then excused herself.

Eve brought out the mugs but decided she wouldn't tempt them with cookies. Coming into the kitchen had been a positive concession since Jack knew Eve associated the sitting room with the first time she'd found herself in the midst of a murder investigation. As an obvious suspect, she'd had to answer some difficult questions.

"I suppose it's too early to ask how Jon O'Brian died."

"Poison."

Her body went limp and the mug slipped from her hold. She tried to catch it, but her reflexes failed and it hit the ground with a loud thud, the broken handle skating off into a corner.

Chapter Five

POISON.

She couldn't get the word out of her mind.

"I walked into a whirlpool of activity. Everyone stood at their assigned workstations. No one spoke. Marjorie, that's Charlotte's assistant, gave me instructions. She had them written down."

Detective Mason Lars checked his notebook. "You say you had the first trays of sushi circulating within half an hour."

She nodded. "And then I got to work on Jon O'Brian's sushi."

"Duck sushi."

Another nod. "He didn't eat fish and I'm guessing he didn't care for vegetables either."

"Some of the sushi had fish."

"Yes. The ingredients had already been laid out for

me. I'm guessing that's as far as the chef got before he became ill." She looked from one detective to the other. "Do you know what happened to him?"

Jack drummed his fingers on the table. "He suffered from a mild case of food poisoning."

"Could he maybe... do you think he might have eaten some of the duck?"

"The duck?"

"I'm assuming that's where the poison was." As far as she knew, none of the others guests had fallen ill, so whatever had killed Jon must have been in the duck sushi. She waited for them to confirm or deny it but neither one responded. "If not the duck... then..." Eve sprung to her feet and walked to the window thinking about all the ingredients that had gone into the sushi. Duck, rice and... "The *pâté*." The chef would have tasted it to check the seasoning. A good *pâté* would have Cognac or Port and that would effectively disguise any foreign substances. Then again, the *pâté* would have been made the day before, at least, leaving no reason to taste it..."

Had the chef made the *pâté*? Anyone working in the kitchen would have had access to it. Anyone living in the house...

Her mind raced.

A myriad of possibilities stormed through her.

Poison. Jon O'Brian had been poisoned.

"Can you tell us how *pâté* is made?"

"I was just going through the list of ingredients in my mind. Let's see," she drew in a deep breath. "There's butter, cream, bacon, shallots, liver, thyme, garlic, salt, pepper, and Cognac or Port wine." She explained the process as if reading from a recipe book.

"I've never had any," Detective Mason Lars said. "Does it have a strong taste?"

"The liver alone has a strong concentrated taste. Very meaty. *Pâté* is heavily flavored, so yes, it does. Any one of those ingredients could be used as a camouflage."

"For?"

"Fish gone bad?" Eve suggested. All the ingredients had been kept in separate plates. If the *pâté* had been contaminated with bad fish, it would have been deliberate. Fish or some other foreign substance.

Not food poisoning, Eve.

Poison.

"Did you taste any of it?"

"I should have. Normally, I would have, but I didn't."

"Why not?"

Pressure, Eve thought. "Everything had been prepared. Even the rice had been cooked. All I had to do was roll the sushi. Charlotte had very precise instructions. The chef would have followed them. I didn't even think about interfering with what had already been set in motion. As far as I knew, I was only part of the production line, dealing with the finishing touches. And..."

"Yes?" Jack asked.

"I found myself in a stressful situation and that's saying a lot because I'm used to pressure cooker stress. This was right out of my comfort zone. The air felt thick with tension. If anything went wrong, someone's head would roll. I've worked in many kitchens and I can tell you, I've never experienced so much stress in my life... and something else. I sensed fear. Charlotte wields a great deal of power. I can almost imagine any one of those people working in the kitchen thinking she could destroy their careers."

"Did you ever feel threatened by her?"

She looked at Detective Mason Lars and tried her best to silence the teenager who'd been hurt so many times by Charlotte's darts of criticism. "No, why? I... I haven't had anything to do with her in years."

Detective Mason Lars exchanged a look with Jack. "But you were in contact with her. She came into the restaurant you owned in New York once."

She looked at Jack. She knew he had to maintain his professional integrity. She couldn't assume anything she said to him would remain confidential.

"She made some scathing remarks about the food."

"Ouch. How did you respond?" the detective asked.

The fact the detective had tried to inject some humor into his tone didn't register until several seconds later.

Eve smiled. Then she realized her smile could be perceived as a response to her thoughts. Someone who'd received a bad rap might have lashed out in retribution. If not then...

Vengeance was a dish best served cold.

"I shrugged it off."

"That's hard to believe."

"I had been prepared for the worst. Charlotte appeared from out of nowhere. I hadn't invited her to the restaurant opening. That would have been enough reason for her to feel slighted."

"She came with a restaurant critic."

"She always knows how to play her cards. Unfortunately for her, the critic had ethics and wouldn't bend to her will. However, that didn't stop her from commenting about the decor. I actually agreed with her. Too streamlined. My then husband had insisted we use a modern look. I didn't argue but I always felt it wasn't welcoming enough." She sat down again. "That all happened several years ago. Then her wedding invitations started arriving. If she hadn't cornered me in town, I would have pretended they'd been lost in transit."

"Invitations?"

"I received about five of them. Three within one week."

"That sounds excessive."

Eve didn't comment. She'd already said enough about Charlotte to paint a clear picture.

“What about the people you met last night? Did anyone say anything to raise your suspicions?”

“About?”

“Bad feelings about the groom.”

“Hard to say. Although I noticed they weren’t playing nice.”

“What do you mean?”

“Like oil and water. Her guests weren’t mixing with his, and that was a statement in itself.”

“Are you suggesting her friends disapproved of her choice?”

She nodded. “And don’t ask me why she chose him.”

Detective Mason Lars frowned.

Eve sensed the question coming her way. “He wasn’t her usual type. I’m guessing he hailed from a different background. Not so affluent. Maybe working class. Then there’s the physical aspect. The man was a head shorter than Charlotte. She had always flaunted these amazing men and here she was with someone who would have looked comfortable in a construction site working heavy machinery.”

Mason Lars took a sip of his coffee. “Maybe she fell in love.”

Eve hadn’t thought of that.

How inconceivable could it be?

“No. She had... has her standards. They’re ingrained. Nothing would budge them.”

"Did you speak with anyone at length?"

"My conversation with Winthorpe would have been the longest."

"Is that his first name or last?"

"Both. He only goes by one name." And she'd give anything to be a fly on the wall when the detectives tried to question him. Winthorpe's monosyllabic responses would have Mason Lars lunging for him.

With nothing more to squeeze out of her, Mason Lars put away his notebook.

"Do I smell fresh cookies?" he asked.

"I made some this morning. Would you like some?"

The detective exchanged a look with Jack.

"I'll put some in a bag for you to take," Eve offered.

"I have some news."

Eve frowned at Jill's hushed tone. "Where are you?"

"On my way over to your place."

"Why are you whispering?"

"There are eyes and ears everywhere. One can't be too careful."

Eve didn't feel in the mood to be made fun of. "Cue laughter?"

"I'm serious. I heard about what happened. Everyone is talking about it."

"How did it get out?"

"The usual way. I told you, there are eyes and ears everywhere."

Eve gazed out at the bay and tried to get her breathing to match the gentle rhythm of the waves. Her stomach felt as if she'd poured cement inside it. Nothing she did could budge the sensation. "So, what's this news you're dying to tell me about?"

"Some of the guests came by yacht. A prestigious car hire company delivered some cars for them to get out and about."

"How did you find that out?" Jill didn't own a car and refused to use her mother's SUV because it came with too many conditions including cleaning it after using it and the marina was too far to walk to from her place.

"The walkers, Linda Brennan and Steffi Grant. They went by the marina."

Eve wondered if Jill had inadvertently discovered the island's trigger for the gossip grapevine. She'd never heard anyone accept responsibility for starting a rumor.

"I'm at your back door." Jill waved.

"Come on in." Eve put away her cell phone and bent down to pat Mischief and Mr. Magoo. "I'm surprised you're concerned about anyone overhearing you. You've got these guys to alert you if anyone comes near you."

"They can't tell the difference between a butterfly

and a person." Jill looked toward the kitchen. "What? No baking?"

"I can't keep a single thought in my mind. I'd probably end up rubbing butter into salt instead of sugar."

"I guess that means you're not up to running through what happened."

Eve sat on the edge of the couch. With a huff, she stretched out on it and stared up at the ceiling. "I'll give you a brief rundown." She gave Jill a bullet point list of events. "Bottom line, there's a killer at large. Again."

"Poison. That's wicked."

"Wicked as in good? I can't keep up with current expressions."

"Wicked as in evil. You know, like a dark witch's doing. Are they sure it wasn't an accident? Someone could have put in the wrong ingredient."

"That's wishful thinking. Whatever killed Jon O'Brian had to be potent and act quickly. The police were definite about it. He was poisoned. I don't think the duck was off. No one else got sick, so it can't have been anything that went into the regular sushi." Eve pressed her hand to her forehead. "I feel responsible."

"Why? Once the duck sushi left the kitchen, you had no control over it."

"You think someone got to it then?" No, not likely, she thought. The waiter would have been in on it. Unless he was distracted. Eve sat up. Could she remember his face?

"Did they say what sort of poison it was?"

"If they've identified it, they didn't mention it to me." Had someone sprinkled it on the sushi after it left the kitchen? Or did they get to the ingredients beforehand? Someone in the kitchen must have noticed something. They'd all been working attentively on their tasks, but Eve knew from experience you could be chopping onion with a sharp knife and still keep an eye on everything and everyone around you.

"We should research poisons," Jill suggested.

"We're not getting involved."

"You said that last time and we ended up right in the thick of it."

"This time it's different. I doubt Charlotte will want me hovering around asking questions. That is, if I find anyone prepared to talk to me. They think I'm guilty. I saw it in their eyes."

"That's shock talking. You're exaggerating."

"No. They lapped it all up. They would have loved it if I'd been handcuffed and dragged away." Charlotte's jet setting friends would have taken her fifteen minutes of fame and spread it far and wide during their travels.

"So what now?" Jill asked.

"We wait for the police to do their job and hope they get it right, meaning... I don't want to go to prison for a murder I didn't commit."

"How about going for a drive?" Jill asked. "It'll do you good to get out of the house."

"Let me guess, you want to drive up to the marina."

As they strode by the marina office, Eve pulled her cap down and quickened her step. If the marina manager caught sight of her, she'd have to explain her reasons for being there...

"Eve Lloyd?"

So much for remaining inconspicuous. "Hi, Nelson. How's everything with you?" She'd met the manager a couple of months before when she'd been digging around trying to find information about a murder victim who'd had his yacht moored at the marina. At the time, he hadn't had any idea she'd been using him to pin down one of the suspects.

"As you can see, I'm busy keeping an eye out on that lot. I don't want anyone falling into the water drunk."

She knew the marina occupancy was dynamic and changed regularly but one glance was enough to pinpoint the newcomers. For starters, their yachts were fancier. "Are they partying?"

"Since lunch today."

"How many yachts are there?"

He chuckled under his breath. "Five. Do you have a special interest in them?"

"No, why would I?"

His smile widened. "News travels fast."

"What have you heard?" She wouldn't mind knowing if the story had retained its integrity or if people were enhancing it. To her surprise, the details were sparse. There'd been a cocktail party. She'd prepared the sushi. The groom-to-be had died.

"I'll let you know if I hear any more news," Nelson offered.

She didn't ask why he thought she'd want to know. Instead, she waved and moved on to join Jill who'd walked on ahead. To Eve's surprise, she was talking to a couple of people from one of the largest yachts.

As she approached, a cheer broke out.

"Here's the woman of the hour," one of them said when Eve caught up with Jill. "Come on up and join us."

Eve was about to say no when she caught sight of Jill's eager smile.

"Just for a minute," she said.

"Thank you. I've never been on a yacht."

"Everyone, Eve Lloyd is aboard."

To her horror, cheers erupted. These were Charlotte's friends...

"This is worse than speaking ill of the dead. Where's their sympathy?"

Someone standing next to her laughed.

"Did I say something to amuse you?"

He handed her a glass of champagne.

"No thanks, I'm driving. Care to tell me why you're all celebrating a man's unfortunate death?"

"You didn't know Jon O'Brian."

"No."

"Then that explains it."

Chapter Six

"WHAT ARE YOU DOING?" Jill asked as she watched Eve spread several sheets of paper on the table.

"Making a list." Eve sat back to gather her thoughts.

Jill laughed under her breath. "How about I make the coffee for a change."

"Sorry, did you say something?" Thug, Eve wrote at the top of the page. "Hoodlum, bully, hooligan. These are all the words used to describe Jon O'Brian."

"And you're wondering what that means? I'd say it was obvious."

"Disadvantaged background springs to mind, but Allan Albright hinted at not so humble beginnings." In the hour they'd spent on the yacht, she'd lost count of the number of times his glass had been topped up. Everyone had been indulging and the flow of champagne had been endless. "Jon O'Brian had been educated in the most prestigious schools but despite his parents' best efforts, he'd chosen to delve into the seedy underworld of something or other. Allan wouldn't say."

"He must have been talking about the nightclubs," Jill said.

"Where did you get that from?"

"One of the guys I talked with. I forget his name. It had a number at the end. Oh, and the guy with only one name said the same thing."

"Winthorpe."

"Yes, that's the one. Imagine going through life with only one name. What does he do when he has to fill out official documents? Where does his name go? First... last. Or ditto, ditto."

"That's the hazard of being unique. You invariably have to explain yourself," Eve said.

"I suppose Picasso got away with it and I'm sure he never had to explain himself. Leonardo, Michelangelo. Madonna."

"What else did Winthorpe say?" Eve asked.

"He referred to Jon O'Brian as a wannabe gangster."

Power hungry. Manipulative. It almost made her think Charlotte had found her perfect match.

"Jon O'Brian was universally disliked. Is that a fair assumption to make?"

"Yes," Jill agreed.

"Let's think about reasons. Snobbery comes to mind. He was different. Not like them. These are the type of people who inherited their money. They have standards. Rules. Expectations. And for some reason, they never care for new money."

"Money's money."

Eve shook her head. "There's a difference. Old money holds prestige. It has a depth of meaning. You're born into it and shaped by everything it provides. Hence the expectation. Pedigree is a vital factor."

"Entitlement?"

"Precisely. But... fortunes dwindle away." Eve thought of the massive fortunes made at the turn of the century and with each generation, the money thinned out. "You've heard the saying it takes three generations to lose a fortune."

"Money," Jill mused.

"Do you think Jon might have held something over them? Like... debts. Or some sort of underhanded activity they didn't want anyone to know about."

"No one cares about that stuff," Jill shrugged. "People thrive on being strange. They even celebrate it. Nowadays, it's all out in the open. That's what social media is for."

Regardless, Eve decided to add a dollar sign and blackmail to her list. "That sort of does away with the whole concept of skeletons in the closet." She drew a little skull and bones on the page. "Hardly any of them are married, so it can't be the risk of exposure if they have an affair."

"Drugs could be a possibility. He owned nightclubs. It sort of goes hand in hand," Jill offered.

"Drugs," Eve wrote and drew an arrow next to the word. "Why am I thinking drug testing?"

"I'd think about that too but you and I are normal. If we drink and then get in a car to drive, we'd worry about being pulled over. Are we digressing?" Jill asked.

"Let's play with it."

"Hang on. I heard a couple talk about board meetings. What if they have to answer to boards?"

Eve perked up. "You might have something there. I know of a few people who don't work but they have to appear to do so. They hold prestigious positions in companies. And some of these companies require their employees to keep themselves clean... drug free. I read about that somewhere."

"So they abstain?"

"Not necessarily. Somehow, they fake it. I wonder if there's a black market for urine samples?" Eve cupped her chin in her hand.

"Feels good to play around with ideas. Even if some of them are way out there." Jill stretched. "And as much as I enjoy these brainstorming sessions, they can be draining. I need this coffee."

"How do you feel about going back tomorrow?"

"To the marina?"

"Yes."

"What's on your mind?"

"I'm guessing they're going to party until they're allowed to leave. I wouldn't mind having a few photos. It'll help to keep track of who said what."

"I hope the coffee's okay." Jill set a couple of mugs on the table. "I don't know how many scoops you put in."

Eve tasted it and hummed her appreciation. "This will make me buzz." As she sipped her coffee she thought about the people who'd been partying in the yacht. It still felt macabre to celebrate someone's death. "Winthorpe looked happier than he did at the cocktail party. I wonder if he feels like a winner. He certainly looked it."

"I'd look like a winner too if I had a yacht like one of those, or drove a flashy convertible. Or didn't have to worry about how to make my weekly income stretch until the following week."

"I'm sure they worry, but on a different scale. The high life doesn't come cheap."

"Maybe Jon O'Brian was a loan shark."

"And he wanted to legitimize his business so he proposed to Charlotte McLain from the Upper East Side." Eve shook her head. "It sounds a bit far-fetched even to my own ears. We're working on a suspect list, not a Hollywood script."

"What do you have so far?" Jill asked.

"One murder victim universally disliked and a bunch of questions I don't know how I'll get the answers to if Charlotte catches on to the fact I'm snooping around her friends."

"I wouldn't call it snooping. They invited you."

"She's not going to like that one bit. She's already decided to make me a target. I'll be lucky to get out of this with my freedom."

"We'll have to make sure she doesn't find out." Jill chuckled.

"What's so funny?"

"Jon O'Brian holding something over Charlotte and forcing her to marry him."

"She'd never let someone hold that much power over her." She wouldn't, but what if someone she cared about had made the mistake of becoming involved with Jon? Not every silver spoon came with an endless supply of money. Did Charlotte care so much about someone other than herself she'd make herself vulnerable to someone else's will?

Eve turned her attention to filling up another page.

"Poison," Jill read.

"You're right, we need to do some research. Find out what sort of poison can act effectively without being detected by taste. Or... something that can be easily masked. Also, it has to be easily accessible. Not something that can only be found in the Himalayas and costs an arm and a leg to buy."

"Why not? Any one of those people could afford it."

"You're right. And it's too early to start excluding possibilities."

"Does this mean you're going to try to catch the killer?"

"It means I don't want to go to prison."

Eve didn't remember seeing Charlotte's parents at the cocktail party, but that didn't mean they hadn't planned on attending the wedding.

Or did it?

If they had disapproved of the match, and chances were they had...

Would they take extreme measures?

She plumped up her pillow and sighed. As keen as she was to find answers, Eve had planned on spending the day plotting out a trip to estate sales the following week. Also, she wanted to figure out a way to buy the most perfect oven for her inn without breaking the bank.

She lay in bed waiting for the sun to rise and tried to clear her mind of all the intrusive thoughts she'd taken to bed with her, but the moment she tried to steer her focus to happy thoughts, the events of the last couple of days surged through her mind.

All those invitations Charlotte had sent her.

She had been keen... desperate for Eve to join in the festivities.

"Or be at hand to become her scapegoat."

She'd been quick to point the finger of blame. To single her out as the one and only person with enough reason to want to harm her.

Why did you do it? Do you hate me that much?

Did Charlotte really believe Eve would seek her revenge by committing murder? On some level, she had to know how nasty she'd been, always putting Eve down because otherwise she wouldn't be able to enjoy her good fortune. People like Charlotte could only be truly happy if someone else wallowed in misery.

"Am I capable of belated retribution?" Sure, Charlotte had made life difficult for her, but the effects hadn't been long lasting. After graduating, they had gone their separate ways. Eve had flourished and had found her passion in cooking and that, in turn, had opened her up to a new world, meeting likeminded people. Competition had been stiff. Sometimes her friends had vied for the same jobs, but everyone had played fair. It would have been an entirely different story if Charlotte had gone into the same line of business.

Eve shivered. That would have been a nightmare.

Why did you do it? Do you hate me that much?

The tension in her voice. The slight quivering of her words. The strained look on her face. She had sounded convincing enough for Eve to now wonder if she could be capable of seeking her revenge on her old nemesis.

She tried to dig up some sympathy. After all, Charlotte had lost her fiancé. There was nothing unusual about her behavior. Of course, she was going to lash out and point fingers of blame. She'd been driven by emotions. Either that or Charlotte had put on an award winning performance.

"I'd hate to see her on the witness stand." Eve raked her fingers through her hair. "Eve Lloyd always had it in for me," she said in her best Charlotte impersonation. Everyone would believe her. She'd know exactly what to wear to court. She might even hire an image consultant. "Let's hope it doesn't come to that." Because she knew Charlotte would pull it off.

A performance...

A ruse aimed at maneuvering Eve into position so she could take the blame.

Her shower did nothing to dislodge the intrusive thoughts. And while brainstorming sessions opened her eyes to possibilities, they also bogged her down with too many thoughts.

When she sat down to breakfast, she played around with her bacon and eggs, moving them on the plate. Then she used her wedge of toast to map out her steps at the cocktail party. Her arrival. Being herded around to meet the guests. Stepping up to the plate and saving the day. She revisited the tension she'd felt in the kitchen. The atmosphere had been intense with it. Had it just been about the pressure of getting everything right for a demanding customer? Or had there been something else, a sense of foreboding?

Jack had asked her if she'd seen anyone acting suspiciously. She couldn't answer that with any degree of honesty or certainty because her memory of the night had become diluted by her feelings of guilt.

She had no reason to feel responsible for Jon O'Brian's death.

So why did she?

"Because I should have stood my ground." She'd had no intention of going to the wedding, but she'd allowed herself to be railroaded. Manipulated. Coerced. Yes, but...

With or without her there, he would have died.

As she finished her breakfast, she heard Mira shuffling around her office. "Would you like me to make you something to eat?" she called out.

"Yes, please. That would be lovely."

"Are you going to eat it if I do?"

"Sorry, did you say something?"

Looking up, she smiled at Mira who'd come into the kitchen. "I thought you were diving straight into your writing."

"I will in a minute but you've enticed me with the promise of food. I know I'll do better if I have a proper breakfast."

"Good. I need to keep busy. Sit down, I'll have it ready in a minute." She organized the ingredients and utensils without giving it much thought. She could do it all blindfolded. Eve knew she'd never add something that didn't belong into her food.

"So where are you at with the investigation?" Mira asked.

"Why does everyone think I'm investigating? I'd never be so presumptuous." Eve gave an impatient shake of her head. "I'm not going out of my way to delve. If something happens to fall on my lap, I'll happily share it with Jack. After all, it's his job." She slid the eggs onto a plate and added the crispy bacon. "Although..." She sighed.

"What?"

"Well, I already have a foot in the door with Charlotte's friends. I'm tempted to see what else I can find out." She chuckled. "Heavens, they hailed me as a hero at the marina. They think I've done the world a favor."

"By poisoning Jon O'Brian?"

"The obvious answer is yes, but that would imply I am guilty of actually poisoning him. Remember, I need to be careful what I say. If I allow something to slip out in private, it could happen when I'm out and about in public."

"I think you should give serious thought to coming on a cruise with me. You need to relax before the last few months begin to take their toll."

"I'll keep it in mind," Eve said, "At least this time I don't feel my life is in danger."

"I thought you said Charlotte had threatened you."

Eve cringed. "Thanks for the reminder." Last time she'd been threatened, she'd worried about Mira coming to harm. "Jill and I are spending some time at the marina today so if anyone wants to come after me, I will have lured them away from the house." She cleared the breakfast dishes and wiped down the kitchen counter. "There's some roast in the refrigerator if you get hungry."

"Do you have a strategy in place?" Mira asked.

Should she? It sounded like a sensible next step. "I'll be testing people's loyalty to Charlotte. I'm guessing their dislike of Jon O'Brian will make them more willing to share information. I only have to be careful they don't catch on to the fact I'm sticking my nose where it doesn't belong. Jon O'Brian had some sort of power over them. I'd like to know what it was."

Chapter Seven

"THERE'S something different about you today. I can't put my finger on it." Eve climbed out of her car and signaled for Jill to turn around.

"Give up?"

Eve nodded.

"It's my yachting gear. Cable sweater. White jeans. Walk the walk type of thing. I want to blend in."

"Good thinking." Eve tugged the sleeve of her seen-better-days sweater that had doubled in sized over the years and wondered if she should think about a wardrobe makeover. As a chef tucked away behind the scenes, she'd never had to worry about her clothes but working at an inn, she'd have more contact with the public. Also, it wouldn't stop with a change of wardrobe. She'd have to start getting her hair done on a regular basis...

"What's with the frown?" Jill asked.

"I like being me, so much so, I never bother to change for other people. You know... to fit in. But I might have to bend a little."

"Sometimes I think you've been living under a rock."

"I'm in transition mode," Eve said, "Setting up the inn will be a huge leap for me. Bear with me and don't be surprised at the changes you'll see in me."

"Let me know if you need me to hold your hand," Jill offered.

"I can tell you right now, I'm going to need feedback from you. I've never been much into fashion." She could hear laughter coming from one of the largest yachts. "They don't sound as loud as they did yesterday. They must be working up to it."

"Any last minute instructions?"

"Yes, be a sponge. Absorb everything you see and hear. Engage anyone and everyone in conversation. I'm going to try to see what else I can get out of Allan Albright." Eve checked her watch. "I hope he's drunk enough to loosen his tongue but not enough to make him incoherent." They were welcomed aboard with another cheer. Within seconds, they both had glasses of champagne in their hands. Eve took a sip and decided that would be enough for her.

She edged toward the most animated group and tried to eavesdrop on the conversation.

Allan Albright stood by the sidelines. Twice, she caught him watching her. In his mid-thirties, he looked like a regular poster boy used to daily pampering and maintenance. Her ex-husband had followed a rigorous schedule, working out at his exclusive members only gym, getting a massage, having a sauna, eating at the finest restaurants... A life without challenges, Eve had thought.

"You look pensive."

She must have been lost in thought since she hadn't noticed Allan Albright moving toward her.

"You must be itching to get out of here. Have the police mentioned how long you'll have to stay on the island?"

He gave a small shake of his head and took a sip of his drink. "We don't mind."

We? His co-conspirators?

"What if you're needed elsewhere?"

"The Bahamas can wait. This is much more entertaining."

His tone had changed from the day before. Eve noticed a hard edge to his words. Almost a stubborn streak. She imagined someone celebrating Jon O'Brian's murder and then wanting to stick around to see how everything panned out because...

Because there was more to come?

She looked around them. "Where are the other guests staying?"

"The O'Brian lot?"

He sounded dismissive, Eve thought and decided to stick with her old money, new money theory. It had to be at the core of the intense dislike she sensed. And resentment went hand in hand with it. "Yes."

"At the house."

"And you're all staying on your yachts by choice?"

He answered with a deep-throated chuckle. "If we stayed at the house, we'd have to go on a starvation diet."

She must have looked mystified.

"A man was poisoned in that house."

"Where's your trust?" she said lightly. Reason told her if Allan had been in on the poisoning, he wouldn't have anything to fear now.

"Haven't you heard? There's a killer on the loose."

Those, Eve decided, were not the words of a major player in this murder. She studied his handsome face and wondered what he had to lose or gain by Jon O'Bri-an's death. Too early to exclude anything... or anyone, she reminded herself adopting the guilty until proven innocent tactic.

"You know Charlotte is going ahead with the events she planned for the week."

Eve could not have been more surprised. "Is she up to it?" It was the first question that came to mind but then others followed. It seemed to be in poor taste. A blatant disregard for propriety.

"She wants to put on a brave face. Life goes on. He would have wanted her to get on with it, and all that jazz. I don't know how she's going to pull it off. Half the chefs she hired walked out."

"They were allowed to leave the island?"

"On condition that they could be easily contacted. Something that doesn't sit well with us. If they can be trusted, why not us?"

"Allan, you have yachts. You could take off for parts unknown and never be seen or heard from again. Of course they're going to insist you hang around."

"Do you think we'd walk out on our lives?"

"Not you, but the killer would. Yes, I'm suggesting it could be one of you." She watched for his response, but he simply shrugged.

"And you're not shy about pointing the finger."

She smiled. "I'll be fine so long as I steer clear of food or drink."

He tilted his head. "How did you get cleared of any wrong doing? From what we hear, you have a long history of being bullied by Charlotte."

"That's the first time I've heard anyone be honest about her."

"We all know what she's like."

"And yet you came to her wedding." Did they fear her? Suddenly, Eve imagined the roles reversed. Jon O'Brian became a victim, someone forced to play along and do Charlotte's bidding and when he threatened to break free of her hold over him... whatever that might have been, she retaliated with poison. Maybe killing her fiancé had been her way of sending everyone a message.

See what I'm capable of doing?

She sent her gaze skating around. What if all the guests had been bullied into coming? At school, everyone had thought they were friends, but Eve had had no choice in the matter. In public, Charlotte had been friendly enough, but in private her snide remarks had taken little bites out of Eve's confidence. Mira had suggested she might have changed over time, but what if she'd only become worse? Taking her manipulative skills to a higher level, employing them to secure a circle of friends she could control.

"You're smiling."

Eve widened her smile. "I just had an amusing thought."

"Share."

"What would Charlotte do if you all walked out on her now?"

He tipped his glass back and emptied it.

The longer he took to answer, the guiltier he'd be. Of what, she had no idea.

"Why would we do that? She's our friend."

The insincerity of his words stunned her. If he'd expressed some sort of confusion, she might have believed him.

Walk out on our friend? What a ridiculous notion.

But his response had lacked all feeling.

"Here comes the Happy Breeze," Allan said.

Everyone looked in the direction of a yacht making its slow approach. Bigger than any of the others and judging by the rise in murmurs, owned by someone everyone had been waiting for.

"A late arrival?"

"Dante Hildegard."

Eve knew the name carried a great deal of meaning, to everyone else but her. Everyone here belonged to the upper echelons of society but it might as well be a subculture for all she knew about their lives and where they came from. They weren't even celebrities one could easily identify from their regular appearances on the front pages of gossip magazines. She might have known more if she'd hung out at international polo matches, private cocktail parties and weekend affairs.

"Hildegard, of the international investments group?" A vague memory crawled around her mind. She'd heard her ex-husband mention him.

"The very one."

Super wealthy and friends with royalty, which put him on an even higher level. "And is he always fashionably late?" Either that or he'd deliberately kept himself away until the deed was done. Suspicion sprung up. Dante Hildegard, mastermind of a plot to do away with Jon O'Brian, pulling the strings from a safe distance. Think motive, Eve, she could almost hear Jack say.

“He does as he pleases,” Allan said.

“Is that resentment or jealousy I hear in your voice?”

“A bit of both. Some people are immune.”

“To what?”

“Need.”

Allan didn’t give her the chance to ask for another explanation. Excusing himself, he disappeared below deck.

Immune from need? She supposed financial security and power made one immune from need.

One can never be too thin or too rich.

She let the quote bounce around her head.

Even people with money wanted more. More of everything. And when the excitement of having enough money lost its luster, they moved on to acquiring more power and more control.

She tried to play around with the idea but again it all seemed to be beyond the scope of her understanding. Eve led a small life, happy to do her job, to enjoy small pleasures in life. She would never consider entertaining herself by making someone else miserable.

She didn’t think any of these people would be thrilled by the challenge of setting up an inn. What thrilled them? What made their hearts pump a little faster with excitement? The thrill of the chase?

As she looked around her she had no trouble picturing them as hunters. Predators.

Eve had hoped the party would move onto the new

yacht, but everyone stayed put and Dante Hildegard didn't make an appearance.

After a light luncheon, the party mood mellowed. Food tended to do that. Feeling she'd gathered enough information to mull over, she called it a day.

On the way home, she exchanged notes with Jill. "Everybody was excited to see the new yacht. Apparently, Dante Hildegard is the life of the party," Jill said.

Why would he come now? Unless he had a solid reason to be pleased about Jon O'Brian's murder, he'd have no excuse.

"The other guests are holed up at the Stevenson's house. I wonder how they're being treated. Charlotte didn't even get around to introducing them to me at the cocktail party because her chef fell ill and disrupted everything. If she hadn't forced me into the kitchen, I get the feeling she would have found an excuse to avoid introducing me to her fiancé's friends." Eve pressed her fingers between her eyes. "Today was a waste of time."

"Let's hope Jack is having better luck. Have you heard from him?" Jill asked.

"No, I was hoping he'd be more open about the type of poison used to kill the groom."

"You missed your turn."

"I didn't have any lunch. How about we stop somewhere. With any luck, we might encounter some of the other guests out and about. Allan said if he'd been forced to stay at the Stevenson house he would not have eaten for fear of being poisoned. I don't know if he was joking or seriously concerned about his life being in danger."

They went into the Chin Wag Café and found a table by the window. At a glance, Eve saw a couple of people she thought she recognized from the cocktail party. People she hadn't been introduced to.

Cynthia Walker, the owner, came to take their orders. "Have you heard any news about what went on at the Stevenson's place?" Eve asked by now accustomed to news spreading like wild fire on the island.

"A couple of the kitchen staff had lunch here before they left the island. They sounded relieved to be out of that house. The guests were appallingly rude and the owners no better."

"The Stevensons?"

"They've lived here all their lives but have never come into my café, so I wouldn't know if that's an exaggeration. You might want to ask around at Shelby's Table. They've been known to have lunch there."

"Why would I do that?"

Cynthia looked slightly confused. "Because you're trying to put two and two together."

"I'm just as curious as the next person."

Cynthia and Jill exchanged a look of amusement.

"Oh, for heaven's sake, stop it. I don't make a habit of snooping around," Eve said in her defense.

"But you do have a knack for getting results."

Not deliberately, Eve thought and turned her attention to the menu. "I'll have your lovely vegetable tart, please."

Jill shared a conspiratorial smile with Cynthia. "That's Eve's way of changing the subject."

Even as Cynthia moved away, Eve could sense her still smiling.

"Did you actually hear anything worthwhile back at the party?" Eve asked Jill.

"A couple of the women were saying how relieved they were about Charlotte finally being free."

"That sounds significant."

"It depends on how you interpret it."

Eve nodded. "Had Charlotte been in an impossible, difficult to get out of relationship or did her friends simply disapprove of the match? We could go around in circles all day with that. Unfortunately, the only person who has answers thinks I killed her fiancé." Eve looked up and saw Allan Albright and Elizabeth-May walk into the café. They were deep in conversation. Elizabeth-May looked animated. Eve might even say agitated.

"I don't care what she says, I'm not going back there. No amount of money is worth—"

Allan tugged her elbow and gave Elizabeth-May a warning look.

Just as it was getting interesting, Eve thought. "Money is at the centre of this," she murmured, "It has to be. We need to get a solid lead on Jon O'Brian's activities. There must be a way to find out about Allan Albright's financial situation as well as everybody else's."

"We'd need a team of people trawling the Internet and scanning through every gossip magazine there is looking for tidbits and we still wouldn't get a full picture," Jill said.

"I should stick to what I know." Eve dug inside her handbag and drew her cell phone out.

"Who are you calling?"

"No one just yet." She scrolled through her contact list. "But there are a couple of people I used to work with who might be able to help out with some information. They can ask around for me, find out if anyone knows one of the people who worked at the Stevenson's house. They'll have some inside information. Who knows what they might have seen or heard. I have to find a way to talk to them."

"You're not likely to be welcomed with open arms."

Eve set her phone down. "Maybe there's an easier way. Do you remember the name of the catering company on the trucks we saw driving to the Stevenson's house?"

"I remember liking the script and thinking it was a solid name, don't ask me why. Hang on, it's on the tip of my tongue." Jill clicked her fingers. "Mayflower Catering."

Eve did a quick search for the contact number.

“Is this where you pretend you’re organizing a party?”

“I am setting up an inn. It would be normal for me to want a grand opening party.” Eve shrugged. “I’m only in the planning stages. Getting quotes...Talking to people.”

Chapter Eight

THE MOMENT they entered the Mayflower Catering building, they struck gold. Eve zeroed in on one of the staff and recognized her from the night of the party. Although, she argued with herself saying it couldn't be the kitchen hand she'd seen because this girl wore a suit and sat behind the reception desk.

She looked at the name tag. "Hi, Millicent. Do I know you from somewhere? I feel I do."

A light splash of pink rose to her cheeks. "I have one of those faces. A lot of people mistake me for someone they know."

Eve tapped her chin. "No, I'm sure we've met. I was recently at the Charlotte McLain cocktail party on Rock-Maine Island."

The blush brightened.

"I'm sure I saw you working in the kitchen."

The girl looked around and leaned forward. “I wasn’t supposed to be there. Could you please not mention it?” She straightened and gave her a bright smile.

A woman dressed in a pristine gray suit approached the front desk. “Hi. I’m Lana Bishop. How can I help you?”

Eve introduced herself and explained she was in the process of setting up an inn and looking to possibly... maybe... have an opening party and as she wanted to enjoy it, she thought it would be a good idea to hire out the catering. Of course, the food would have to be a reflection of the fare she’d be offering so she’d have strict guidelines.

“We excel at those and our customers always receive exactly what they expect. What sort of numbers are we talking about?”

Eve plucked a number from out of nowhere.

“Two hundred. We can do that easily and if you don’t have your kitchen set up, one of our trucks is fully equipped.”

“What about staff?”

“We hire only the best. Our chefs are fully qualified with extensive experience.”

“And your kitchen assistants? Are they qualified too?”

The woman lifted her chin slightly. “Of course. We

have inspectors making sure we adhere to regulations. They are all fully qualified in food handling."

She was given a tour of their showroom set up with different table settings and shown a variety of menus. Cost was something that would be discussed when Eve had a better idea of what she wanted.

To her surprise, Lana Bishop didn't give her a hard sale.

"What now?" Jill asked as they sat in her car.

"Now we wait for Millicent to finish up for the day."

"You think she knows something?"

"She worked in the kitchen that night and she said she wasn't supposed to. I want to know how and why. I have a vague recollection of seeing her in the background. If she'd done something wrong, it would have been obvious. Chefs are not known for their patience and someone would have told her off straightaway."

"Yes, but... do you think she'll talk to you?"

"Leverage. I have it. She wasn't supposed to be in the kitchen. She could have been covering for someone, or maybe moonlighting to get extra money. I did it myself when I first started out. We'll know soon enough."

"What about Lana Bishop? She looked suspicious to me."

"We'll ask Millicent about her. If she says anything to raise our suspicions, we'll follow it up then. Remember, I want to talk to the people who worked in the kitchen that night. I think Millicent can give us the foot in the door we need."

They had an hour to wait, but their patience paid off.

First they saw Lana Bishop leave in her flashy little convertible. Soon after, Millicent came out, her head bowed, her shoulders hunched in a way that suggested she'd had a hard day at the salt mines. Eve felt a twinge of reluctance. But she needed to get to the bottom of this and she refused to go home empty-handed.

"Millicent."

She hurried her step so Eve broke into a trot.

Thankfully, Millicent didn't break into a run. Instead, she stopped and swirled around to face Eve.

"What?"

Clearly her customer service amiability didn't extend outside office working hours. Fair enough, Eve thought.

"Were you trying to pick up extra cash that night or covering an absence?" That seemed more feasible.

"Why do you want to know?"

"You weren't meant to be there, Millicent." Playing a guessing game, Eve said, "That could get you into trouble."

Millicent looked around her and pushed out a breath. "I had to drop something off or else heads would have rolled."

Did that mean Lana Bishop was another Charlotte type?

"When I arrived," Millicent continued, "One of the chefs said they were short staffed. I had to find a solution, solve the problem, so I stayed on. He only needed help washing vegetables."

"What did you have to drop there?"

"One of the boxes had been left behind. It should have gone out with the trucks the day before. It was an essential ingredient. I'd been responsible for keeping track of what needed to go that day but I must have missed it. One moment it was there, the next it wasn't. I got side-tracked and I assumed it had been loaded. The truck left and the next day I noticed the box had been left behind. Sometimes it gets hectic."

"And what was in the box?"

"*Pâté*."

"The *pâté*. The poison had to have been in the *pâté*. The box was in the Mayflower Catering office overnight. Anyone could have tampered with it." Eve left the message and disconnected the call. Belatedly, she realized she hadn't told Jack anything he didn't already know. The lab people had already determined the cause of death so that meant they'd found traces of the poison in the *pâté*.

"Jack didn't answer?"

Eve slipped her cell phone inside her pocket. "No,

but hopefully he'll listen to my message and get back to me."

"What if he doesn't? You'll never share information with him again?"

"You talk as if this is going to be a recurring problem. This is it. No more deaths on the island, thank you. We've already had our run of bad luck." She relaxed her shoulders and took in the pretty scenery. The leaves were turning, but there were still some splashes of color, the last blooms of summer. Potted plants still hung on verandas but soon they'd be taken in. Some of the houses had had fresh coats of paint and that would brighten up the cold days ahead.

"It might be like a fad. Island life had been too quiet for too long. Now it's our turn to experience murder and mayhem."

"In that case, I might have to pack up and leave. I don't think I can live in a place where I have to constantly look over my shoulder."

"You'll get used to it. You do realize we're under constant threat of a meteor hitting the earth. But you don't see people walking around looking up at the sky to see if they can spot one. Everyone gets on with the business of living life because the disaster they fear might never happen."

Eve frowned. "Hang on. What about the doomsayers?"

"Do you see anyone standing at the curve holding up a placard, beware, you might be next?" Jill asked.

"I wouldn't joke about it."

"No, I guess not." Jill laughed. "This mental image of you walking around with a sandwich board popped into my head. It's going to be like one of those tunes you can't rid of."

"It could come to that." Eve shook her head. "Honestly, there have been three deaths since I've come to live here." And to think she'd come here to relax...

"Freakish coincidence. Let's hope it has nothing to do with the law of attraction."

"What do you mean?" Eve asked.

"You know, what you think about, you bring about because that would mean you have murder on your mind."

"Hey, why me? Why not someone else on the island?"

"Because you're the newcomer." Jill smiled. "An easy target. By the way, I took some photos of the guests on the yacht. What do you want to do with them?"

"We'll print them up and start a pin board."

"Do we get to draw circles around the main suspects?"

"You sound thrilled."

Jill hummed. "I've had a quiet month."

"I thought you were happy dating Officer

Matthews." The two had paired up when Officer Matthews had been assigned to watch over Mira's beach house when a killer had been on the loose and, since then, they'd become inseparable.

"I was, but he's on a training camp so I haven't seen him in a couple of weeks."

"Sorry, I should have noticed... I should have asked. Does that make me selfish and self-centered?" She had been busy thinking and planning. And once again, trying to get over the experience of having a gun pointed at her.

"You notice other stuff. Don't be so hard on yourself."

Eve brushed her hand across her brow. "I'm not usually. I'm putting it down to Charlotte's presence on the island. She's a force to be reckoned with and has a lot to answer for."

Jill fell silent for a moment, and then she said, "We all have a Charlotte in our lives. Mine was the woman I worked for at the magazine."

A woman who'd turned Jill's working life into a nightmare. She didn't understand why some people had to justify their existence by making other people miserable. It would be enough to drive anyone over the edge... but how far?

What drove a person to kill? Desperation? Greed? Vengeance. "If you had the chance... would you..."

"Plot her downfall?" Jill asked.

"Kill her."

"Let me think about it."

"I guess you wouldn't. If you have to think about it, it means you still have command of your reasoning mind."

"But I could still decide I'd be a happier person if I took matters into my own hands. Of course, by then it would become a premeditated act."

"We'd make dreadful killers."

"Incompetent," Jill agreed.

Eve's cell phone rang. "Jack."

"You sound surprised," he said.

"I am." In truth, she always sounded breathless when she heard his voice. "I didn't expect you to return my call so soon."

"What are you up to, Eve?"

"No need to sound suspicious. I'm parking my car. Now I'm getting out of the car. Walking toward the front door."

"Cute."

She heard what sounded like a sigh of frustration. "I'm baking a chocolate tart if you'd like to come by later on."

"I doubt I'll be able to get away. Now, please tell me you didn't go snooping around the Mayflower Catering company."

"Why would I do that?"

"Because you can't help yourself."

"You seem to have forgotten, so I'll remind you. I'm in the process of setting up an inn and I want to throw a party."

"You're a chef. Why would you hire outsiders?"

"Because I want to enjoy the party and not have to work."

"The answer is yes."

Yes? It took a minute for Eve to figure out what he meant and then she remembered the text message she'd sent him. "So, it was the *pâté*. Did you question Lana Bishop?" She didn't expect him to answer.

"We did but it sounds like you managed to walk away with more information."

"Is my winning way beginning to grate on you?"

"Please try to avoid antagonizing people. They reserve the right to accuse you of harassment."

"I'll keep that in mind, detective. Anyhow, Lana Bishop didn't reveal much. The receptionist, on the other hand, had some interesting information. Did you talk to Millicent?"

This time, she heard a growl.

Eve did a little dance on the spot. It suddenly hit her. They were onto something.

"We narrowed it down," she whooped with joy and then filled Jack in on what she'd found out about the *pâté* being left behind at the office.

"All right, Sherlock."

"You'll have to be very careful how you approach

Millicent. You don't want to spook her. I think she's under a lot of pressure from Lana Bishop and she's probably scared she did something wrong."

"Are you doing an online psychology course? Where's all this insight coming from?"

"I'm only putting myself in her place. Lana Bishop is as bad as Charlotte and Millicent depends on her for her livelihood." Which Eve had now put at risk. If Lana Bishop had anything to do with the poisoning, then she'd go to prison and Millicent would be out of a job. "You need to look further into Lana Bishop."

"Do you have a motive to go with your suspicions?" Jack asked.

"No, but I'll think of one while I'm baking my tart. I'll call you with the results."

She strode into the house and found Jill organizing their notes in the kitchen.

"I hope you were serious about baking that chocolate tart. It's all I can think about now."

"I'll get right onto it." Eve brought out the ingredients. "You could start on a clean page. Put Lana Bishop and her catering company at the top."

"What about Millicent?"

"I think she's an innocent bystander. We can think of her as a witness. Jack asked me about motive. We'll have to come up with something." Lana Bishop drove a flash car. "Did you notice the make of Lana's car?" Eve asked.

"Brand new top of the line BMW."

"Dollar value?"

"A couple of hundred."

"Thousand?"

Jill nodded. "And that suit she wore is expensive too. Right along with her hairstyle. You don't get haircuts like that from your local hairdresser."

So, Lana Bishop's business did well enough to support her lifestyle. Had that always been the case? Eve's restaurant had done well from the start, but she'd employed a marketing guru and her ex-husband had insisted on hiring the most expensive stylist he could find. In no time, they'd become the place to be seen in. It hadn't come cheap. Eve had used her savings and had borrowed heavily. But there were other ways. In fact, at one point her ex had suggested getting investors onboard.

"Let's play with the idea of linking Lana Bishop to Jon O'Brian."

"You do realize we're not professional private detectives."

"That's right. We're not detectives, but we have brains. We can figure this out."

Eve cut up the butter into cubes, measured out the flour and sugar and got to work preparing the short crust pastry rubbing the butter in while she kept an eye on what Jill wrote.

Jill had a wobbly pen moment going. "I'm going

to follow your lead and call on my friends. I used to work with Ellie. She has this incredible system of cataloguing all her magazines. And then there's her photographic memory. It might take her a couple of days, but if she's seen or read something, she'll remember."

"And what do you think she'll be able to come up with?"

"The major social events are covered in the social pages. There might be some mention of Jon O'Brian appearing somewhere. Also, Lana Bishop might have catered some glitzy event. There'd have to be something about her company. Someone who drives a car like that has to be doing the catering for important people." Jill sat back and smiled. "I hope you realize this is a major breakthrough."

The *pâté* had been tampered with. The only way to connect someone would be to find a motive. A solid reason to kill. The killer would have worked out a plot and, most importantly, he or she would have known they could execute it without a glitch. Only a person who thought they were in full control could do that and Lana Bishop struck her as the controlling type.

Eve smiled.

"I guess you didn't see me do my happy dance outside. But it's really too early to tell. Let's celebrate when we have a solid lead." That meant they'd have to dig deep and start making connections. "Lana Bishop has to be somebody of note in the catering world. Otherwise, Charlotte would not have used her."

"Unless it wasn't Charlotte's choice to make."

Back to Jon O'Brian pulling the strings and backing Charlotte into a corner, forcing her to bend to his will because he held the purse strings.

Chapter Nine

LANA BISHOP. Jon O'Brian. The jet setters. Charlotte...

There had to be a connection.

And what about Marjorie?

Charlotte's assistant had come across as a scared little mouse. A prime candidate for a crime of vengeance. Push someone hard enough...

Eve nibbled the tip of her thumb.

"Either you're mulling over something or you're turning against yourself."

"I'm frustrated." Eve picked up the menu, and then set it down again. She'd been in touch with Shelby and had subtly hinted at wanting to know when and if the high-fliers made a booking at Shelby's Table and Shelby had come through that morning saying they'd booked several tables for lunch, but so far, no one had shown up. Her frustration didn't end there. Eve felt they should be concentrating on Lana Bishop. But where to begin? Jill's friend hadn't come through with anything yet but Jill had said it could take her a couple of days to sift through her massive memory bank of magazine articles read over the years.

"Come on, out with it," Jill said.

"I feel we're lacking purpose. Wandering around aimlessly."

"I disagree," Jill said. "We've come up with a few ideas."

Eve gave a slow shake of her head. "We need to start asking the right questions."

"Is that all that's bothering you?"

"No. I don't understand their attitude. Their lack of concern. The way they celebrated someone's untimely death. And the social barriers don't end there. It's them and us. I can't get my head around where they come from. How they live. What they do with their days. I couldn't go through my days doing nothing the way they do."

"You're overanalyzing."

Eve had to agree. "Yes, trying to look beyond surface appearances."

"There's nothing to it. They're enjoying life. They function at a slower pace. A more appreciative one. They have time to smell the roses while the rest of the world rushes around."

"So explain to me how they finance it all? Some of

them are fifth generation and they don't appear to be doing anything to increase their money. Yet we know life is more expensive now than it used to be. And there's more to do. More to have." Money, Eve insisted, had to be a main motivator for murder.

"What's really worrying you?"

The information trickling in was getting mixed up with her feelings. Eve threw her hands up in the air. "I've never envied anyone. A part of me must resent them because I'm not willing to let them off the hook, even after turning our focus to the catering company. I'm not naturally a jealous person. And I don't envy their easy lifestyles. But maybe... maybe I do resent their aimlessness. Do they serve a purpose?" She shrugged. "I'm really fixated with their lack of concern and sympathy. Those are basic ingredients... the makings of a coldblooded killer. Someone from the jet setter's group has to be involved too."

"It could be a group effort."

"All of them in on the conspiracy?" Eve shuddered.

Jill nodded. "Like a club. A killer's club."

Her mind grabbed hold of the idea. "An exclusive club with high membership fees. I like that. I have to write this down. I've no idea what it means, but I think it's part of the puzzle." Eve looked up. "Here they come. Eyes and ears, Jill. We watch everyone and listen to what they all have to say."

They'd done well. Dante Hildegard had come with

the group. Eve made a mental note to thank Shelby for the heads-up phone call.

A couple of people, including Allan Albright, gave her a nod of acknowledgment but she was not asked to join their party. Eve didn't mind. She really wanted to focus on catching something of interest and thought her chances would improve if she didn't lose herself in a conversation.

They didn't have long to wait.

"Someone else will take his place..."

It took Eve a moment to realize the tone had changed from party mode to business. The subject at hand had to be a serious one. But not serious enough if they were prepared to tackle it in public, she thought, unless they were all confident no one would add two and two together.

"It can't happen again."

"Agreed."

Moments later, their tone changed as a waiter came to take their orders.

"Anything but fish."

Whoever had spoken triggered a general consensus. They'd all be steering clear of anything fishy. Their concern should have let them off the hook, but Eve refused to clear them of any wrongdoing.

"Where's your spirit of adventure?"

A brief glance over her shoulder identified the man

as Dante Hildegard. She knew that for sure because the woman next to him mentioned his name.

"Weren't you recently in Japan, Dante?"

"I was. Next time you're there, make sure you try some Fugu..."

Eve's eyes widened. She looked at Jill and mouthed the word. If not prepared properly, Fugu could be lethally poisonous. She drew out her cell phone and sent Jack a text message. He hadn't told her what sort of poison had killed Jon O'Brian but she'd bet anything it had come from the Fugu fish. It could have been snuck into the *pâté*.

Her mind whirled with possibilities.

From one moment to the next, she decided to take the fish out of the equation and leave only the poison. She knew the fish liver had the most concentration of toxin. The liver might have been blended in with the duck liver to make the *pâté*...

But how would they have managed it? She didn't think the fish was available locally. She couldn't be sure, but she suspected it might only be found in the tropics, and not in cold-water climates.

Unfortunately, once they'd made their menu selections they steered the conversation away from food and switched to fashion and yachts and their next destination. Eve noticed no one talked about vacations or time off. She imagined if anyone mentioned the word work they'd have to search a dictionary for the meaning.

"Did you get anything out of that?" Jill asked as Eve hurried her out of the restaurant.

"Only the possibility of the poison coming from a fish that is not even found in these waters. If Jack doesn't get back to me with a confirmation I am going to be annoyed with him. He owes me."

"At least you've perked up."

"I feel we have something to work with now."

"I would have liked to have dessert," Jill complained, "Why did we have to leave so quickly?"

"I can only take so much talk about fashion and yachts. You can have some chocolate tart at Mira's place. Mention of the fish shifts the suspicion back to Lana Bishop. We need to get on-line and see what we can find about her. As far as I'm concerned, she is currently our prime suspect."

Lana had become the strongest connection to the possible source of poison. The *pâté*. Jack would want to know why. Eve decided Millicent had played an innocent role, ignorant of the consequences of taking the box to the Stevenson's house. If she'd left the *pâté* behind, Jon would still be alive today.

Did Lana Bishop have a reason to want Jon O'Brian dead?

"I wish we had some insight into their conversation," Jill said. "Someone else will take his place. I assume they were talking about Charlotte finding a new man. But I can't begin to imagine what they meant by saying it couldn't happen again."

"Let's toss a few ideas around. How about... they thought Charlotte had made a mistake by choosing Jon, a man who didn't belong to their social circle, and they don't want her to make a bad choice again."

"We're assuming her choice of husband would affect them."

"It would. You should have seen them at the cocktail party. Like oil and water, not mixing. They don't take kindly to outsiders. You heard the way they talk. It's as if they have a secret code only they understand. Someone from outside of their circle would make life awkward for them. Come on, we'll figure it out."

"The more I think about it, the less ideas I come up with," Jill grumbled.

"How about we divert our attention with some research?"

It took them several hours to trawl through the current online issues of several magazines but as the clock struck midnight, Jill jumped to her feet.

"I found something. It's an article in a local newspaper. Mayflower Catering re-opens its doors after surviving its financial crisis. The owner, Lana Bishop, has taken over all catering of functions for the Stellar Group owned by Jon O'Brian. That sounds like a significant contract for her."

"You found the connection." Eve clapped her hands.

"Well done. We have a link." Again, she had no idea what the business connection meant, but they had to start somewhere, so she decided to use it as a springboard...

Getting a fresh sheet of paper, Eve drew a pyramid. Charlotte and her friends at the top. Below that, Jon and below him... Lana Bishop.

"Wait, there's more. Brace yourself. The deal was brokered a day before the couple made their engagement official."

Eve shot to her feet. "What?"

"This is dated seven months ago." Jill grinned. "I believe we have a motive... or two. Jealousy and possibly, revenge."

"Are you suggesting Jon dumped Lana for Charlotte?" Eve asked.

"I'd stake my non-existing reputation on it."

"We'll have to find out how they broke off the engagement and... When Jon met Charlotte. When and how did that happen? That way we can draw up a timeline."

"If someone broke up with me and moved onto someone else, I don't think I'd want to have anything to do with them."

Eve thought about it. "What if there's money involved. Lana Bishop had recently resurrected the business. She wouldn't want to take backward steps. But would she bide her time? Wait for the opportunity to seek revenge on the man who dumped her, assuming that's what happened." Eve got up and paced around the sitting room. "She talks Jon O'Brian into convincing Charlotte to have the wedding on the island and to engage Mayflower Catering. For all time's sake. That would have been a big account for her. But she's still furious with Jon for dumping her. With everything in place and going according to plan, she strikes at the most opportune moment. She has a contract so her connection to Jon's company remains intact. Someone else takes over Jon's company and she continues to do the catering for them because no one knows she killed him. I think it's called having your cake and eating it too."

"You're starting to think like a killer."

"Are you afraid to spend the night under the same roof?"

"Now that you mention it... Yes!" Jill laughed. "Are you going to share this with Jack?"

"I'll sleep on it. I'd like to have something more solid. Jack is starting to appreciate my input. I don't want to ruin his new perception of me by giving him something flimsy."

Jill continued to read the article. "The break-up didn't affect their business relationship. And she even picked up quite a few other clients along the way, all with links to Jon."

"So now that she's secured the business contacts,

she strikes. We know the poisoned *pâté* came from her catering company and we assume the break-up left her embittered."

Jill raised her hand. "To be fair to her, anyone in her company could have contaminated the *pâté*. Including the chef who fell ill."

"We don't even know his name. Millicent should be able to help us out. We should try to get as much information out of her as possible before she realizes her livelihood is being threatened. If she thinks we have something on Lana, she might decide to cover for her boss and save her job."

"Or she might wise up and use her knowledge as leverage to blackmail her boss. Give her support in exchange for..." Jill shook her head. "I think I'm getting carried away. Best to focus on the victim and the suspect we already have instead of trying to make someone else a target."

"I don't think Lana would do something drastic if Millicent turned against her. It's all out in the open now. It would be too obvious. Another murder? No."

Eve brushed her hands across her face.

Lana and Jon.

Did Charlotte know her fiancé had been engaged to the caterer?

Absolutely. Yes. Charlotte didn't like surprises so she would have had her fiancé's background thoroughly scrutinized. Eve wondered if she'd confided in a friend, maybe one of the jet setters.

Eve laughed under her breath.

Charlotte wouldn't spread this type of news around and she definitely wouldn't confide in anyone. Charlotte had always known many people but none she would consider friends. Not really.

"I need to speak with Charlotte."

Chapter Ten

THE NEXT MORNING, Eve strode into the kitchen and found Jack studying her notes. She'd almost forgotten how handsome he looked at any time of the day.

"Who let you in?"

"Mira."

She looked over her shoulder and saw the door to Mira's study closed.

"She said she'd been up since the crack of dawn, apparently her duke is giving her some trouble."

The duke who just happened to resemble Jack... "And you decided to help yourself to all our hard work."

"I assume you were going to share it with me."

"Only after Jill and I made any sense of it. I'll put some coffee on. I suppose you'll want breakfast as well."

"I wouldn't say no." He tapped one of the pages.

"You seem to have made quite a case against Lana Bishop."

"Did you know she'd been engaged to Jon O'Brian?" The tightness in his jaw told her he hadn't. "I'm sure you would have found out eventually." She told him all she knew as well as her suspicions, even though they were all over the place.

"So you think Lana Bishop bided her time, set herself up with contacts and contracts and then took her revenge on Jon by killing him."

"It's a safe assumption. She didn't seem to make a fuss when the engagement ended and they remained business associates. She must have set her personal issues aside and put her business first. That makes her single-minded and determined to surge ahead no matter what. Her catering business had been on the brink of failure. She wouldn't let her ego ruin all her hard work."

"How did you find out about the fish?"

She swung around. "Are you actually confirming the sushi was laced with Fugu toxins?"

He nodded. "We found it in the *pâté*.

Eve filled him in on everything they'd overheard at Shelby's Table and agreed with him that all the remarks were open to interpretation. "It can't happen again. They had to be referring to Charlotte's choice of husband. And also implies they have some say in the matter. I'm thinking they might apply peer group pressure so Charlotte doesn't make the mistake of getting mixed up with the wrong type again."

"What do you know about the toxin?" Jack asked.

"I know the restaurant preparation of Fugu is strictly controlled by law. You have to be a qualified chef to prepare it." She'd done some reading the night before but had eventually fallen asleep. "The training is quite rigorous and only about thirty five percent of the applicants pass. Part of the test actually involves preparing the fish and eating it. There have been some rare cases of death. The liver is the most toxic part, but it's banned from use. I don't know what the actual effects are. I didn't get that far."

"The toxin paralyses the muscles," Jack filled in, "The victim can't breathe and eventually dies from asphyxiation. There's no antidote." He raked his fingers through his hair. "You said you tried to perform CPR."

"Yes, but someone hauled me away."

"Who?"

"That's just it. I don't know. A man, but I couldn't say which one of the guests." She put some bread in the toaster. "Would CPR have helped?"

"Hard to say. The *pâté* that went into the duck sushi had a high amount of poison. You might have been able to keep him alive until the ambulance arrived, then it would have been a case of supporting the respiratory system, but like I said, the dosage was high. The medical examiner said a recovery would have been unlikely."

"Strange. I don't feel as bad as I did. I guess I felt guilty for not being able to do anything to save him." Any attempt at CPR would have been futile. She had to believe that or else spend the rest of her life thinking she hadn't done enough. Or rather, she hadn't been allowed to do anything.

"Did you meet Jason Stevenson?" Jack asked.

The owner of the house. Eve tried to remember. "No. I'm sure I didn't. Is he the one who pulled me away?"

"Yes. He was concerned you'd do more harm than good."

Eve strode over to the table and added his name to the list.

"Just like that?"

"Yes. Everyone's a suspect until proven innocent. I've learned my lesson. If Jason Stevenson was in on the poisoning, the last thing he'd want is someone stepping in and trying to save the day."

"Motive?"

"He had money problems. Investments gone bad. He's one of the obvious suspects and should have been on the list from the start."

"And?"

Eve gave a small lift of her shoulder. "He'd be in a desperate enough position to do anything for a quick buck. Which brings us back to trying to pinpoint the person who would have gained the most by Jon's death."

"You have Lana down for crime of passion and revenge."

"Premeditated. Jill and I decided last night Lana would have wanted to feather her nest before finding the right time to strike. We assume Jon dumped her and no woman likes that."

"I'll keep that in mind."

She smiled and caressed his cheek. "You do that."

"So, what are your plans for the rest of the day?"

"I'd like to find out more about Dante Hildegard. He's a dark horse."

"And unknown to us. Fill me in."

"French toast all right with you?"

"Perfect. Need a hand?"

"No thanks." She gestured for him to sit down. "Dante sailed in the other day in his super yacht. Everybody seemed to be in awe of him. I suspect he's wealthier than all of them put together." She whipped a couple of eggs and dunked the toast in. "If I hadn't overheard him mentioning Fugu yesterday at Shelby's Table..." She shook her head. "I'd probably still be waiting for you to share some information."

"Remind me again why I have to do that?"

"In this instance? Because I'm involved. I've been dragged into this and they... he or she tried to make me the scapegoat. I have a right to know, Jack." It didn't surprise her to hear him change the subject.

"Going to the restaurant on the same day the guests were there was quite a coincidence."

"I have my ways, you have yours."

"Yours always sound more attractive and fun. Lunch and parties aboard a yacht. Did you manage to hear anything else we might use?"

"The only significant piece of information we got from that lunch was the fish. Something you could have told us about. It's not readily available here and we now know the *pâté* had been laced with it."

"Thoroughly. Leaving no doubt of its effectiveness."

"How's the chef who fell ill doing?"

"He's recovered and he's gone on to another job."

"And you obviously asked him if he prepared the *pâté*."

"He didn't."

"But you know who did."

"Yes."

"And of course, he pleads ignorance. So that means the *pâté* had been tampered with by someone else. It had to have happened before or soon after it was put away in the refrigerator to set. I'm leaning toward Lana but you want motive."

"It's one of those essential, annoying details," he laughed.

Eve set the French toast down on the table and sat next to Jack. "Help yourself."

"Keep going the way you are and we'll have to make you an honorary detective."

Eve took a bite of her French toast and paused. "I like the sound of that, but I'll have to pass. Thanks. I wouldn't want to get a reputation for solving crimes. It could put me in an awkward position. I could end up being like a gunslinger from the old west. Their reputations made them a target for other gunslingers looking for a challenge. I'm already opening up an inn where a murder was committed. That's enough notoriety for me, thanks."

"You're still worried it'll become the destination for killers on vacation?"

"I can just picture the Killer's Daily Gazette advertising the latest dream vacation spot where even the proprietor has a history of being a suspect." Eve sipped her coffee and took a moment to enjoy sitting with Jack over breakfast. They hadn't done that for a couple of weeks. She missed the company, but she understood he couldn't always get away.

"Good morning," Jill yawned.

"Hope we didn't wake you up. Ready for breakfast?"

"Don't get up. I'll start with some coffee." Jill shuffled into the kitchen and poured herself a cup.

"Jack's impressed with our progress."

"Eve and I want to know if anyone's experiencing money problems. We're widening our net and including as many people as we can in our list of suspects. Hang around us long enough, Jack, and we might include you too."

"And how would you try to pin the murder on me?"

Jill looked up at the ceiling. "You tried to get revenge on behalf of Eve to make up for the years she suffered under Charlotte's reign of tyranny."

"Isn't she smart?" Eve asked. "Help yourself to some toast before they get cold, Jill."

"Did you tell him about the conversation we overheard at Shelby's Table?" Jill leaned forward and mimicked Dante's voice. "It can't happen again."

"We've been trying to make sense of what that might be but the problem with catching snippets of conversation is that we're too biased to fill in the gaps. Anything and everything we hear sounds suspicious."

Jack's gaze bounced between Eve and Jill. "It sounds innocent enough to me. They were referring to the death of someone they knew. That means there's been a breach in security."

"We think Jon was a loan shark and one of them got in too deep. Jack, you need to start looking at their finances."

"It sounds like my workload just increased."

Jill grinned. "Any time you get stuck, you know where to come for answers."

Eve set down her mug of coffee. “Is that why you came here so early? Are you stuck or are you keeping tabs on me?”

Jill topped up her coffee. “My money is on him keeping tabs on you. I haven’t heard him warning you to keep your nose clean.”

“Now I’m worried.” Eve turned to Jack. “I hope you’re not using me as bait to lure the killer out into the open.”

He brushed his hand across her arm. “Anything else I should know about?”

A knock on the front door had them all looking at each other.

“Who could it be this early in the morning?” Eve asked as she went to answer the door. When she returned, she set an envelope down on the table. “You’ll never believe this.”

Jill snatched the envelope and drew out a thick velum page. “It’s an invitation to lunch at the Stevenson place. Today.”

“I’m suddenly feeling faint,” Eve said.

“You have to go, Eve. This is your big chance. How else are we going to know what they plan on doing with you?”

“Are you suggesting they know I’ve been asking questions and are now going to try to do away with me?”

Jill turned to Jack. “We think there’s a group

conspiracy. It's like a secret club." Jill clicked her fingers. "Eve should wear a wire. Or at least have her cell phone on speakerphone so we can listen in on her conversations."

"That's actually not a bad idea," Eve mused.

"Eve."

Jack's warning tone made him sound like a bear with a sore tooth.

"I'll be careful."

The invitation had been unexpected enough to make Eve wary if not concerned. Charlotte had planned something and she needed Eve to play whatever role she had scripted for her. If only Eve knew what that could be. She didn't think too much about it because her focus remained on talking with her and trying to find out how Charlotte felt about her fiancé's previous relationship with the caterer. Eve would settle for seeing Charlotte's reaction, but whatever plan Charlotte had set into motion did not include talking.

Charlotte waved to her but kept a discreet distance. If Eve moved in her general direction, she reclaimed her space. It happened a couple of time. Enough to make it clear she had no intention of engaging in conversation with her. Which begged the question...

Why had she invited her?

Eve checked her watch. She'd never been much of a drinker but if she wanted to blend in, she'd have to play by the rules. Smiling at the waiter, she accepted the glass of champagne on offer.

The magic wand had been waved and all the guests had gathered, including the jet setters. A few of them raised their glasses at her. Eve interpreted this as the standard greeting so she returned the greetings with a lifting of her own glass but she refrained from drinking.

"You look lost."

Allan Albright to the rescue.

"I'm not even going to pretend this is my scene," Eve said.

"Why is that?"

"Why won't I pretend or why isn't this my scene?"

Allan Albright smiled. "Both."

"I'm not out to impress anyone and my bank account balance lacks several zeros to belong to your set."

"That's easily fixed."

"You have a secret to wealth creation?" Not that she cared. Eve's only purpose in life had been happiness. Doing what she loved had always been at the top of her list. If she'd followed in her parents' footsteps, she would have gone into law and pursued a career at international level earning seven figures, but she'd followed her own path and she couldn't escape the fact she'd always have to work for a living.

"There are always ways. The right people open the right doors."

"I guess I could always marry money."

"There's that too, but..." He sighed.

"Let me guess, money marries money?"

He shrugged. "It's a fact of life."

She forgot she'd decided she wouldn't drink and took a sip. There were only so many wealthy people in their circle to go around... "Doesn't it get incestuous?"

"If push comes to shove, there's always new money."

Is that what Jon O'Brian had been? "As a last resort?" He nodded. "You are a picky lot."

"Ouch. Are you implying we're snobs?"

"I'm saying it, not implying it. You didn't even try to hide your dislike of Jon O'Brian."

"Like I said, if you'd known him, you would have felt the same way."

"What made him so... unpalatable?" She cringed at the subtlety of the word. What would Jon O'Brian have said? She imagined a string of expletives pouring out of him.

"His crassness."

She'd been right.

"Has someone been rude to you?"

Eve swung around. Dante Hildegard came to stand beside her. He held a drink in one hand, and a golf club in the other.

"We haven't met."

Allan introduced them.

"Do you play golf?" Dante asked.

Eve looked into his dazzling turquoise eyes. "Never in my life." And she had no intention of starting now, not even for the sake of spending more time with a good-looking man. He stood a head taller than her and had the sort of sex appeal that guaranteed he'd never spend a night alone.

"Not even for the sake of walking and talking?"

How could she refuse?

"When exactly does the walking part begin?" Eve asked as she settled into the golf buggy.

"I'm told there's an uninterrupted view of the ocean at the edge of the estate."

She hoped he didn't mean the cliff.

Her stomach sunk.

He meant the cliff.

"You're Charlotte's friend from way back. Why haven't we met?"

"We move in different circles."

"Pity." He brought the buggy to a stop and hopped out.

She watched him set up his shot and take a swing. "Where's the fun in hitting balls into the ocean?"

He gave a nonchalant shrug. "I want to hit a few balls but not worry about collecting them."

No thought given to the environment. His blatant negligence set her back teeth into a hard clench.

He gauged the light breeze and then took another shot. “You live on the island year round?” He didn’t wait for her to answer. “That would do my head in. It’s cooling down. Perfect time to head down south were it’s warmer.”

“I like the coziness of a fire.”

He went on to tell her about all the places he’d stayed at in the last few months, turning the one-sided conversation into a tour of the world’s finest restaurants.

She saw her opening and went for it. “I suppose there’s no point in craving a life I know I can’t afford.”

“Who says you can’t.”

“My bank statement.” She expected him to deliver a generic platitude about money not being everything. Instead he surprised her.

“Your aunt is a bestselling author and you’re her only heir.”

And how exactly did he know that? Had he asked around or had she been screened? Eve realized she’d been too blasé about her aunt’s safety. “And your point is?”

“Her books will continue to sell long after she’s gone.”

Meaning, Eve would have a steady source of income. Only a few months before someone had used that as an excuse to kill. It wasn't even something Eve ever thought about...

"You'd want to make sure you're free to enjoy it."

Free...

Eve laughed. "Are you trying to tell me something?" Or was he threatening her? And if so, why?

The hardness of his eyes made her take a step back. She was about to take another when it occurred to look over her shoulder. Another step would take her right up to the edge of the cliff...

Chapter Eleven

"JACK. Two visits in a week. You're in the middle of a murder investigation. You don't usually have time for me." Eve frowned. "Hang on. You found something... and shock of horrors, you're here to share it with me."

He smiled and for a moment, Eve's breath caught.

"You didn't call yesterday so I assume you didn't discover a new suspect."

"No." It had taken her the best part of the night to forget about the disturbing conversation she'd had with Dante Hildegard.

"Is there a but in there somewhere?"

"I had the feeling I was being interviewed." Or blackmailed.

"For?"

"I spoke with Dante Hildegard. He painted an

enticing picture of his lifestyle. It almost sounded like a sales pitch."

"And you rushed home to pack your bags."

"Afraid you'll lose me to the high life?"

He tilted her chin and held her gaze. "I might have to put this guy on my suspect list."

His smile sent her heart skipping around her chest. "Anyone else might have salivated but I didn't find any of it interesting. Maybe I imagined it, but I thought he was on a recruiting drive. Although I have no idea how I'd fit into the scheme of things." She explained how Dante had singled her out and how Charlotte had avoided talking with her. Had she been invited for the sole purpose of having a face-to-face talk with Dante Hildegard? "I wish I had more for you."

"It's not as if you're on the payroll, Eve."

Thank goodness for that. She didn't think she'd survive the constant stress. "So, what really brought you here, detective? You know if I had anything worthwhile I'd share it with you."

"I'd actually appreciate your input. Your mind..." he shrugged. "It works in mysterious ways. You see things that would never occur to us."

"Come in."

They strode through to the kitchen. "Would you like some lunch?"

"No thanks, I've already eaten."

"If you don't mind, I'm going to finish mine. I

didn't have any dinner last night and I'm in need of comfort food," she said and took a bite of her grilled cheese sandwich.

"Busy brainstorming?"

"Something like that." She'd actually tried to switch off and stop thinking about suspects and killers on the loose. "So, what's on your mind?"

"Some information has come to our attention."

"You were serious." She couldn't hide her surprise. Jack had been warning her to steer clear of suspects since they'd first met. Had he finally accepted the fact she had an inbuilt magnet for trouble?

"Charlotte's father lost a considerable amount of money."

Eve surged to her feet, the words spilling out of her like a volcanic eruption, "That's it. Charlotte had her hand forced. She had to agree to marry Jon."

"Are you all right?"

She shook her head. Taking a deep breath, she sunk back down on her chair, probably looking as deflated as she felt.

"That was quite an explosion."

She tried to laugh it off. "Honestly, that's been sitting in the back of my mind for days. My head feels like a terminal station with trains clogging up the system. I haven't been able to speak with Charlotte so I have no idea what drove her to pick someone like Jon."

He brushed his hand along her back. "Feel better now?"

"Much, thanks." She gave herself a moment to calm down. "Okay, tell me what else you got."

"From what we understand, Charlotte doesn't work. It would be safe to assume she had to find a new source of income."

Eve agreed. "She wouldn't be happy about daddy cutting off her allowance, or even cutting it back. She's like the eye at the top of the pyramid. Everyone beneath her has to prop her up." Eve stared into space, eyes unblinking, thoughts whirling around her head.

"What?"

"That's it. Skimming," she whispered.

"What about it?"

Again, she surged to her feet, but this time she strode around the room, her steps slow. "Returns on investments are dropping. Less money coming in. Standards of living on the rise. More money needed."

Jack looked lost.

"Sorry. I'm used to doing this with Jill. She usually jumps in and adds to the mix or tries to make sense of what I've said." She held up a finger. "Jon O'Brian was a wannabe underworld boss and how do these guys make their money? Extortion. They skim. They take a percentage. He must have had dozens of businesses under his so-called protection. Let's imagine there are other ways of reeling in a new source of income. Like sponsorship. Help someone to get themselves on their feet and get a return for your investment."

"Lana Bishop."

Eve nodded. "I'm willing to bet there's no proof of her taking out a loan from a bank to re-establish the catering business. Instead she went to Jon and he helped to bring her back from the brink of bankruptcy. He didn't do it out of the goodness of his own heart. There had to be something in it for him. A percentage of takings."

"I like what I'm hearing."

But that still didn't give her the answers she wanted. Or the motives Jack needed. "This is annoying. It's like trying to think of a word and it sits on the tip of your tongue but refuses to take shape." She glanced at the sheets of paper on the table stacked one on top of the other. Layers of fact and fiction.

Eve frowned.

"Did you just think of something?"

"Yes, I think I have but this is where I entertain way out there possibilities."

Jack nodded. "Go ahead."

"Charlotte's desperate to retain the status quo of her life. She's forced to marry for money. But she's smart. If she marries someone from her inner circle, she risks facing the same circumstances of... what's the term... diminishing returns." She pumped her fist in the air. "She thinks she needs to introduce new blood. Yes, new money. While she has her standards, she's smart enough to know she can make a small sacrifice for long-term gain."

"You think she planned on divorcing Jon O'Brian?"

"Most likely. Although, he'd be smart enough to set up a prenuptial agreement of sorts. Charlotte wouldn't like that." She stopped. If Charlotte didn't like something, she found a way to make it work for her. "Jon must have had a significant dollar value for her to consider marrying him." Eve bit her lip and tried to digest the difficult conclusion. Charlotte's long-term plan included killing her fiancé...

And framing Eve for it.

"You're hesitating. What's wrong?"

Pointing the finger of suspicion at Charlotte was easy enough. But how would Charlotte have pulled it off? Had she somehow tampered with the *pâté* herself? "I'm stuck." She lifted her shoulders and as another thought struck, they lowered. "Changing subjects at the rate of knots. Jill and I had this idea about a club and membership fees. Belonging to the jet set club requires a huge chunk of money. Let's say, you're wealthy enough to maintain a descent standard of living, but you're rich and you want more. You want to rise to another level. To mix with an even better pedigree of people. Dante Hildegard is one of those people. He has entry into royal houses."

Jack's eyebrows rose.

"I know. It's a world we don't know anything about or even understand, but it exists. Anyway, Dante can facilitate entry..."

"At a cost."

"Yes. Like everyone else, he has his own skimming company. He takes a percentage fee from people wanting to rise to another level in society." She waved her hand. "Of course, he must have serious money stowed away in the Caymans or wherever super wealthy people put their money, but he'd never turn his back on a money spinning idea. I'm thinking Jon O'Brian might have paid a fee to enter Charlotte's world. But something went wrong. No one approved of him. So, they... collectively... decided to get rid of him."

"Are you saying they're all in on it?" Jack brushed his hand across his chin. "I don't know about that."

"I told you it was way out there." She held up her hand. "Hang on a sec. I need to think about something else."

"Out loud please."

"You'll mock me."

"I wouldn't dare."

"All right. Here goes. What if Charlotte became Jon? Not literally. She steps into his shoes. She becomes the extortionist, skimming off the surface. She realizes she doesn't need to marry Jon after all, so she does away with him."

"Are you suggesting she cut out the middle man?"

"Yes."

"Why not end the engagement?"

"This is Jon O'Brian. A tough guy. A gangster. He calls the shots. Who knows what he was capable of? I can only assume he wouldn't like being pushed around and he wouldn't take it sitting down. Charlotte loves her shoes. They come in all shades but concrete gray."

"But why go to the trouble of poisoning him?"

Eve clutched her stomach. "To frame me." And it had backfired. "I'm surprised she hasn't lodged an official complaint about me not being put behind bars."

"Who says she didn't?"

"Why didn't you tell Jack about Dante threatening you?" Jill asked, her eyes wide with concern.

"Because... because I might have imagined it. I've become so fixated with this murder my mind can only perceive shadows and murderous intentions." She growled under her breath.

"You need a holiday."

"I suggested she come on a cruise with me," Mira offered as she helped herself to another cookie.

"What I need is for killers to stay away from the island. We don't want it becoming an infestation."

"There's a town meeting in a couple of weeks," Jill

said, “You could suggest posting a guard at the bridge. Only good people get to drive through.”

“A check point. That’s a great idea.”

“I’ll leave you two girls to sort out the security of the island. My duke requires my attention.”

Eve waited until Mira had disappeared into her study to suggest they go out for a walk along the beach.

“I think it’s time to lure the killer out.”

Jill dug her heels into the sand. “You did not just say that.”

Yes, she had. And she’d needed to say it because she needed Jill to talk some sense into her. She shouldn’t get involved... put herself and others at risk. This had nothing to do with her. Let the professionals handle everything. But... She was involved. She’d been dragged into it kicking and screaming.

“We’ve reached a stalemate.”

Jill wagged her finger at her. “Then we step back and let the police do their job.”

They walked along in silence. Eve tried to enjoy it for as long as she could, letting her thoughts float around without focusing on any one of them. But then one rose to the surface and caught her attention.

Do you hate me that much?

Charlotte’s rage had been driven by emotions. Either that or it had been a performance and now Eve had to wonder how Charlotte could hate her so much. She could understand an emotional outburst but not one that had been perfectly planned and executed.

Hate didn't come into it, she reasoned.

Charlotte didn't have time for emotions. They didn't serve any purpose.

Eve broke the silence. "Who's our strongest suspect?" She didn't see Jill roll her eyes but she knew she had by the droning tone of her voice.

"Charlotte McLain."

"Who has the most to lose?"

"Everyone. Their freedom, their lifestyles and their ill-gotten gains."

"Who's the most desperate?"

"My finger is still pointing at your school buddy, Charlotte."

"Who is the most cold-blooded?"

"How do you measure that?"

"You're right." Eve folded her arms and looked out to sea. "We don't have resources. Jack can look into their finances. He can tap their phones, he can check banking records... so long as they're not in some offshore account or a Swiss bank. He can find out where they've been, where they're going. We're limited."

Jill sighed. "Only by our imaginations. It's fun trying to put two and two together."

"You don't have to sound so defeated."

"Can't help it. But I guess the old adage applies. If you can't beat them, join them. And this is fun."

"Yes, but let's not forget someone died because someone else killed him." Eve gave a firm nod and rubbed her hands together. "We need to stir things up."

Jill groaned.

"Use the island grapevine to spread a rumor."

Jill's groan died down to a whimper.

"Let's see... How about, I've found proof and I'm mapping out a trail leading to the prime suspect. That should bring the killer out into the open."

"You want to set yourself up as bait?"

"Do you have a better idea?"

"Yes. Let Jack do his job. Throw yourself into your inn. You said you wanted to go to estate sales. Or we could become couch potatoes and watch daytime TV at least until the killer is caught."

Eve stopped and swung toward Mira's house. "My only concern is involving Mira and you, of course."

"I can't believe you're serious about this. Is there anything I can say to change your mind?"

Eve knew she had to tread with care and be smart about this. She had to position herself... Be strategic. "I know what I'll do."

"I guess the answer is no."

"Sorry, did you say something?"

"Nothing compelling enough to change your mind."

"As you pointed out, I haven't done anything other than buy a house which I'll eventually turn into an inn, so I can't hold an opening party but there's nothing that says I can't hold a pre-opening party. Like a rehearsal party. And I want to do it now while Charlotte is still in town. That way, I get all the major players to congregate in the same place."

"Where?"

"The inn."

Chapter Twelve

"I'D LIKE to commission some paintings from you for the inn."

Jill did a double take. "Are you trying to distract me or get me out of the way?"

Both, Eve thought as she studied the entrance to what had been Abby's house but now belonged to her. Lock, stock and endless repayments.

Eve remembered the day she'd seen the for sale sign posted outside Abby's bookstore. She'd only recently come to the island for a brief visit but had been thinking about her prospects and what she would do with herself after selling her restaurant. There were still days when she thought the house had been an impulse purchase triggered by a need to find any excuse to remain here with her aunt. Mira didn't really need her around but Eve had come to realize she needed to experience the feeling of belonging she'd enjoyed when she'd been younger and had come to spend her summer vacations here.

"I won't insult your artistic integrity by suggesting size or color. I trust your judgment and taste."

Jill pinned her with a raised eyebrow look. "How considerate of you. So, I suppose you now want me to scuttle off to my studio and stay there while you go out of your way to taunt a killer into taking action."

"I promise I'll keep you up to date."

Jill folded her arms and lifted her chin. "I'm not budging."

"Suit yourself." Eve strode into the house and began opening windows.

"What do you mean?"

"This place needs airing."

"Eve?"

"If you want to hang around, then by all means do. I'm going to spend a few minutes in each room and decide what I'll keep and what needs to go." The house had come fully furnished with antiques. It had added to the cost but Eve couldn't turn her back on pieces that had been here since the house had been built. She strode into the dining room and swirled around. "I love the wallpaper but it needs freshening up." The tiny daisies were faded as was the pale green in the background. She suspected it was meant to be more green than gray.

"There are some places that specialize in reproductions," Jill offered, "If you can't source it, they'll make it for you. And yes, I'm trying to show you I can be helpful."

"You'll always be my sounding board."

"If there's a but in there somewhere I don't want to hear it."

"You'll thank me later," Eve said under her breath and swung toward Jill. "I think I've taken on more than I can chew here. Painters have to be organized. Wallpapers sourced. The floorboards checked. I want to retain the quaintness of the house but not the creaking floorboards. A couple of the windows will need replacing. They're stuck. The list is endless and I can't be in all places at once. How would you feel about visiting some show rooms and collecting samples for me?"

"I'd hate it because I'd know you were only trying to get me out of the house and out of harm's way so the answer is no."

"Fine. You're determined. Although, not very long ago you would have jumped at the opportunity to get out and about and away from—"

"Mischief. That's all this is and I'm telling Jack."

"All right." She pursed her lips. "I won't do the party."

"Promise."

"You're determined to shadow me so how am I supposed to organize it all without you knowing?"

"You can be devious."

"I give you my word. I—" A knock at the front door cut her off. Eve didn't move.

"Are you expecting someone?" Jill asked.

"No."

"Then there's no reason to answer it."

"But it... it could be a neighbor." Eve took a step but Jill blocked her.

"Or it could be Lana Bishop because you can't help yourself."

"I promise you, I have no idea who that could be."

"Why don't I go answer it then? I know this isn't my house, but you have such a heavy workload, I want to do all I can to help ease your load." Before Eve could stop her, Jill rushed to the front door. Moments later she returned, a smug smile in place. "Look who's here."

"Lana... Hi. W-what a lovely surprise."

"I'm sorry. Did I get the dates mixed up?"

Eve tilted her head and smiled. "Dates?"

"I'm sure you said to meet you here today—"

"Oh, yes. Of course. Come in." Eve avoided meeting Jill's disapproving gaze. She'd explain later. She hadn't lied or misled her. She'd... forgotten to cancel. Eve made a mental note to remember that excuse. "Let's go into the sunroom. It's lovely there at this time of day." Jill followed them, her expression mulish.

Eve couldn't help noticing the elegant cut of Lana's suit. And the shoes. She'd have to ask Jill about them but she didn't need to be a fashion expert to know they were expensive. Eve shifted in her seat and tugged at her old pair of jeans. Her clothes were intended for comfort but they could be a statement. She saw nothing wrong with dressing down. Living on the island, she didn't have anyone to impress.

Leisure wear, Eve.

Jill's voice floated in her mind. She'd worked for a fashion magazine so she'd know all about making the right fashion choices even when you didn't intend stepping out of the house.

"Have the numbers changed?" Lana asked.

Eve tried to pick up the thread of the conversation. Her gaze strayed over to Jill who stood leaning against the door, her arms folded, her eyebrows lowered into a slash of disapproval.

"You mentioned inviting two hundred people."

"Oh... yes. That sounds about right."

"What about the invitations. We can also include that in our services."

"I'll have a list drawn up." Did she even know two hundred people?

Lana looked around the sunny room. "This is very... cozy. Were you thinking of having the party indoors?"

"Do you have any suggestions?"

"You could have both indoors and outdoors. You could also have one or the other. The weather is still mild enough to hold it outside. We have a selection of marquees to choose from."

Was there anything Lana Bishop didn't supply? Eve felt tempted to ask about Fugu but decided that would be teetering too close to danger. She sifted through the barrage of questions she needed to ask and remembered the key one. Did Charlotte know she'd been engaged to Jon?

"I didn't notice the marquees when I visited your office."

Lana gave her a tingling laugh. "We outsource."

That would provide her with the perfect set up to skim off other companies. It seemed every shark had a small fish to feast on.

"Some of our customers have very specific tastes, so sometimes we have to have something designed and made specifically to order. For instance, one of the last parties I catered had an Arabian Nights theme so all the marquees were designed to look like Bedouin tents."

"I doubt I'll want anything so specific."

"But you'll be particular about food," Lana said, "You mentioned that you wanted it to reflect your menu."

She had?

"Yes. Of course." Seeing Jill roll her eyes, Eve gave her an impatient shake of her head. "Did Charlotte McLain suggest the menu or did you have an input?"

Eve mentally growled at herself. She'd meant to work up to that, not spring it on Lana Bishop.

"She's one of my favorite clients. Knows exactly what she wants."

"So you'll still be doing business with her," she said, her tone hitched up to express surprise.

Lana gave her a small smile. "Of course."

"No hard feelings about your sushi killing her fiancé?" She didn't wait for Lana to answer. "I've never known her to be so tolerant and forgiving."

Lana Bishop's face remained expressionless. "We've been cleared of any wrongdoing. The police are no longer questioning us."

"That doesn't mean they've crossed you off the list," Eve said.

"Me?" This time, her voice broke and she visibly stiffened.

That could be a natural reaction, Eve thought. She'd clearly put a lot into revamping her business and a mishap such as poisoning one of the guests could ruin her.

"Take it from someone who's been there. Once a suspect, always a suspect, until the real culprit is discovered."

Lana lifted her chin, clearly determined to proceed despite her slip up. "What happened to Mr. O'Brian was unfortunate."

"Mr. O'Brian? I would have thought you'd be on

first name terms. After all, you were engaged to him. Or did I hear wrong?"

"Who told you that?"

Eve's eyes widened into what she hoped would be perceived as an innocent expression. "I thought it was common knowledge."

When Lana straightened Eve realized she must have crumbled a bit at her line of questioning.

Good, she was getting to her.

"It wasn't common knowledge."

The remark sounded flippant, as if she now didn't care one way or the other. Eve wondered why Lana didn't bother to deny it more fiercely. A real killer would be well versed in covering their tracks.

"Not common knowledge? I thought I read about it somewhere. In fact, I know I did." Eve clicked her fingers. "I scan through so many newspapers every day I can't remember exactly where I read about it. These days, my attention is focused on local businesses, so it must have been a local newspaper. I can see why you'd think no one would know about it." By no one, she meant someone like Charlotte McLain who wouldn't bother with inconsequential small town gossip. Eve knew she'd hit the jackpot. "Charlotte doesn't know."

A fierce splash of bright red appeared on Lana's cheeks.

Her fingers twitched. Her lips pressed down slightly.

Eve wouldn't be surprised if she surged to her feet and stormed out. But she didn't.

"I'd like it to remain that way."

She spoke so softly Eve nearly missed what she'd said.

"I can be discreet."

"I'd appreciate that." Lana checked her watch. "I can see you're still in the thinking stages. If there's anything I can help you with, don't hesitate to contact me." She collected her handbag and got up, her legs, Eve noticed, giving a slight wobble.

She'd hit a spot.

"How far in advance would I need to make the booking?" it occurred to ask.

Lana Bishop opened her mouth to reply and then hesitated. Almost as if she'd suddenly remembered something. "As a matter of fact, we're fully booked until next month."

"Would you be able to squeeze me in?"

"Unfortunately, no. There's so much to organize. We prefer to be thorough."

A month? By then, Charlotte and her friends would have moved on. She didn't think Jack would take that long to find the killer and Eve would be stuck with a party she had no intention of holding.

"We'd also require a deposit up front." Now Lana sounded more confident.

"How much?"

"Fifty percent."

"That's hefty. Is that usual?"

"It is for first time customers."

Yet something told her she'd just made that up, as a way to discourage Eve from going ahead with the party and perhaps prodding for more information?

She didn't give her a chance to question the fee. Finding her stride, Lana made a beeline for the front door, gave her a brief wave goodbye and left.

"I don't think she wants my business."

Behind her, Jill chortled. "What do you expect? Did you see how she reacted? I think you've made an enemy."

"What? How?"

"If she has to choose you over Charlotte... do you need me to spell it out for you? I bet you anything if you call her now and set a definite date for the party she'll suddenly find she's fully booked out for the next dozen years."

"My money's as good as Charlotte's. If not better. I'm a local. Charlotte won't be around to hold any more parties on the island. It would be in Lana's interest to bend over backward for me."

"And yet, I'm willing to bet she's already decided she doesn't want anything more to do with you."

Eve swung on her feet and went in search of her cell phone. Moments later, she huffed out a breath.

"Well?"

"She didn't answer. I left a message saying I'm willing to pay the full amount upfront."

By the next day, she still hadn't heard back from Lana Bishop.

At precisely nine o'clock that morning she dialed her number. Again, her call went to voice mail. Fine. She left a message. "Lana. It's Eve Lloyd. I was hoping to hear back from you today. I'm on my way out and will be meeting with Charlotte McLain so she and I can talk..." She paused, "I might be able to pick her brain about some things. You know, woman to woman. Call me." She hadn't lied. She hadn't even fibbed. While Charlotte had made it clear she didn't have the time of day for her, there was nothing to stop Eve from having a conversation with her, albeit in her head.

She expected Lana to be smart enough to realize when she was being blackmailed. Eve's silence about her engagement to Jon O'Brian in exchange for her catering services.

"I guess that means I'm really having a party."

And how exactly would she coerce Charlotte into attending?

Chapter Thirteen

"IT'S the same time it was a second ago when you last checked your watch. I thought you said you'd earmarked today for the estate sales. Are you running late for something?" Jill asked.

"And I thought you'd rather stare at your thumb than spend your day looking at antiques." If Jill knew they'd been hot on Dante Hildegard's heels since she'd first spotted him going into an antique store an hour before, she'd be grumbling about putting their lives in danger.

Jill shrugged. "Someone has to keep an eye on you."

"It's all you've been doing all morning. You're making me look suspicious, almost as if I can't be trusted in a roomful of expensive antiques. Will you look at the price of this vase?" Eve picked it up and looked at the bottom. "I'm starting to think I'm sitting on a gold mine. There are stacks of this type of knickknacks at the inn, but I never bothered to take a proper look."

"They must be worth something. You certainly paid enough for them."

"It was worth it. Think of the time I've saved. If I had to furnish that house from scratch I'd never get the place open."

"Why are you suddenly in such a hurry? I thought you were going to take your time. Suddenly you're pretending you want to have a party and everything else needs to happen yesterday. You don't even have a kitchen and that's the first thing you talked about doing up."

"I've looked at ovens."

"Have you even advertised your inn... hired staff... contracted a linen service?"

She hadn't thought about any of that.

"You haven't. In fact, I don't know why you keep referring to it as an inn. It's still a house. And at this rate, it might stay a house."

"In case you haven't noticed, I've been otherwise engaged—"

"Sticking your nose where it's bound to land you in trouble. You're waiting for Lana Bishop to return your call. Admit it."

Eve chewed her bottom lip. "So, what if I am?"

"I bet you don't even know why you want to have her catering your fictional party."

"To gather all the suspects in one place and play them off against each other."

"You plucked that out of thin air."

"Rounding up the suspects is a good idea," Eve said, "In fact, I think Jack should organize a re-creation of the night."

"I'm beginning to think you have a death wish." Jill gave a slow shake of her head. "Come on. There's nothing here."

Eve nudged her in the ribs.

"Ouch. What was that for?"

"Don't look now, Dante Hildegard is at the other end looking at an antique mirror."

"Why tell me he's here if I can't look. Did he just walk in?"

"Promise you won't get mad at me," Eve said.

"I've done mad. Now I'm simmering and waiting for the inevitable explosion."

"I saw him at the first store we went into."

"And you didn't think to share that with me because..."

Eve shrugged. "You would have dragged your feet. We had to remain inconspicuous."

Jill grumbled under her breath. "Are you going to tell me when I can look?"

"Turn discreetly and slowly. Pretend you're looking at something."

"Is that who I think it is?"

"Who? Where?"

"Striding up to him."

"Lana Bishop." Making her way toward Dante Hildegard. Were they meeting for the first time? In an out of the way place, Eve thought.

"I guess this means she has a legitimate reason for not returning your call. She's busy with a bigger fish."

Eve drew in a shaky breath and looked around her. If she wove her way around the store she might be able to get close enough from the other end without being detected and listen in on the conversation. If either one saw her, Eve knew she'd have a legitimate reason for being here. The same couldn't be said for them. This looked like a clandestine meeting. They were up to no good. She could feel it in her bones.

"Eve, I've got a bad feeling about this. I think we should leave."

"I'm not going home empty-handed."

"At this rate, you might never go home. You don't know what these people are capable of."

"I'm glad you see that."

"I'd have to be blind or stupid not to. Look at the way he's pretending to be looking at that table while he's talking to her. And she's doing the same. Talking but not looking at him. It's so obvious."

"You stay here. I'll be back in a second."

Jill grabbed hold of her arm. "It's not worth it, Eve."

She was about to argue when her cell phone rang.

Eve checked the caller ID. Her eyebrows lifted. It took all her willpower to not look in Lana's direction. "Hello, Lana. How lovely to hear from you." She looked at Jill and raised her eyebrows. As she listened, she took hold of Jill's arm and signaled for her to follow her out of the store. "I'm not sure I'm free. Let me check my diary." She checked her watch. "Okay. I can be at the inn in an hour. I'll see you then." She disconnected the call and scooped in a big breath. "She wants to see me to talk about a proposal."

"I don't like the sound of that," Jill said.

"Neither do I. Yesterday she suddenly became unavailable. She avoided my calls. Today she meets with Dante and now she wants to meet and talk. I'm guessing whatever she has to say has nothing to do with catering."

"What are you going to do?" Jill asked.

"I'm going to go see Charlotte."

"You won't get a foot in the door."

Jill was right, but she had to do something. "I suspect the other day she invited me at someone else's request. Dante Hildegard is calling the shots and I aim to know what his end game is."

"If you think he masterminded Jon's death, you'll have to come up with a motive. Remember, Jack likes motives."

Eve got in her car and tapped the steering wheel.

"You're making me nervous. Talk to me."

"Hang on a sec." She got her cell phone out again and dialed. "Charlotte. It's Eve. I need to talk to you." She listened to the silence on the other end. "It's important," she added. She heard Charlotte's intake of breath. When she agreed to meet her, Eve released the breath she'd been holding. "Okay. Meet you at the inn in an hour." She gave her the address and hung up.

Jill grabbed hold of her seat beat. "Buckle up, this is going to be a bumpy ride."

"I have one more call to make."

"Please tell me you're calling Jack."

"Of course, I'm calling Jack. Do you think I'd throw myself in at the deep end without a plan?" Her call went to voice mail. "Jack. It's Eve. I'm meeting Charlotte and Lana at the inn in an hour."

"That's it?"

"I can't drag him away from work. If he thinks I'm in any danger, he'll send a squad car."

"You don't feel the slightest bit guilty about tapping into police resources?"

"Not if I catch a killer."

"Yeah, that's the part I haven't caught up with. How exactly do you plan on doing that?"

"It is called taking matters into my own hands. Don't quote me, please. We need to see what happens when Charlotte and Lana are in the same room. I gave Lana the impression I had let the cat out of the bag by passing on sensitive information to Charlotte."

"About Lana being engaged to Jon?"

"Yes."

"You're evil."

"Keep up, Jill. I did no such thing."

"Lying is just as bad."

"Not if it's for a good cause."

"My mother told me there's never an excuse for lying, not even to spare someone's feelings. There are ways around it."

Eve sighed. "You're missing the point."

"I'm actually trying to make a point. There is never an excuse for meddling in something that could get you killed."

Eve nodded. "And I count on you to always remind me of that."

"I see there's no talking you out of it," Jill said under her breath.

"I'm going home to change. We'll have a quick coffee and go to the inn."

"What's wrong with the clothes you're wearing?"

Eve gestured with her hand.

"Sorry, I didn't quite get that. Note to self, learn to read Eve's hand gestures."

"Next to Lana, I feel like a poor country mouse. You have to help me choose some more appropriate clothes."

"You? Feeling self-conscious? I never thought I'd see the day."

Eve spent the drive home trying to picture the scene

she'd set but didn't get further than the shock and anger on Charlotte's face at being forced to confront something she would prefer to ignore.

"Put the kettle on, please. I won't be long." Eve said as she rushed upstairs to change. When she reached the top landing, she waited to hear Jill in the kitchen and then snuck downstairs and out the front door.

Guilt weighed heavily on her as she drove to the inn. She had no idea what she'd be walking into, but she knew for sure she didn't want to put Jill in any danger. It had already happened a couple of times and she couldn't bear the idea of being responsible for anything happening to her.

She knew she'd get an earful afterward. But she'd deal with that when the time came. However, when she pulled into the driveway, she caved in and called Jill.

"You're not going to like this," Eve said.

"And you're not going to like what I did," Jill grumbled.

"What did you do?"

"The moment I discovered you'd left without me, I called Jack and guess what? He's on his way. If you think you're in trouble with me, wait until he gets his hands on you."

"Do me a favor and stay with Mira. I didn't like Dante's tone the other day. I'm sure there was an underlying threat there. If anything happens to Mira, I'll never forgive myself."

"This isn't going to end well, Eve. You're taking on two dangerous women. One of them is most likely a killer. What if they're both killers?"

"They're not going to try anything in front of witnesses," Eve assured her.

"You obviously haven't thought this through. What if they're collaborating?"

"I'm not sure that's the right term to use. But you're right. They might be in cahoots. I promise to be very careful and not turn my back on either one. I have to go. There's a car coming." Eve disconnected the call and waited for the car to pull up.

To her surprise, it wasn't Lana or Charlotte.

Millicent.

She strode along the path, her head lowered as if in deep thought.

As Eve pushed her car door open, another car pulled up.

Again, Eve waited. And again, she was caught off guard.

Allan Albright.

Two people Eve had delegated to the bottom of her suspects' list.

This couldn't be a coincidence.

She sent Jack a quick message alerting him of the changed circumstances.

She got half way up the path when she heard a car

drive off. Turning she saw it was the car Allan had arrived in. There had been someone else with him.

A quiver of apprehension crawled along her spine. She tried to shake the sensation away by thinking about motive and opportunity.

She gazed at Allan and Millicent as they stood on the front veranda chatting. These two were not the major players. It had to be Charlotte or even Lana. They both had a long list of motives and they'd had plenty of opportunities to dabble in a bit of poisoning.

Don't shoot the messenger, Eve. She could imagine Millicent being coerced into making an appearance, as for Allan Albright...

He too would be acting on someone's behalf.

Who pulled his strings?

Charlotte or...

Dante.

"Hello, Allan. Millicent."

When Allan turned to face her, he slanted his gaze toward Millicent.

Eve frowned. And then she looked down.

Millicent held a gun pointed directly at her.

"Inside. The both of you. Don't make me repeat myself."

Millicent?

Sweet, chocolate covered Millicent who'd begged her not to say anything about working that night at the cocktail party?

"Allan, what's this about?"

"Why are you asking him? I'm the one holding the gun."

"Is it even real? It looks like a toy to me."

"Um, Eve." Allan shook his head.

Allan stood more than a head taller than her, dressed in tailored pants and a white shirt that showed off his sculpted body to perfection. While Millicent wore a dark blue dress matched with blue heels that looked to be about three inches high. Even so, she was more than a head shorter than Eve. Yet she held a gun and she spoke with a menacing tone.

"What are you even doing here?" Eve asked. "I have an appointment with Lana Bishop not you."

"Which part of I have a gun don't you get?"

"I don't know what your game is, Millicent, but let me tell you right now I've had bigger guns pointed at me and I'm still standing."

"You think this is a joke."

Eve turned to Allan. "What are you doing here?"

"Charlotte just dropped me off. I convinced her you had nothing to do with poisoning Jon O'Brian and talked her into coming to make peace with you, but at the last minute she changed her mind."

"So you don't know anything about this." She nudged her head toward Millicent and her gun.

"I have a fair idea."

"One you're hopefully going to share with me."

"Isn't it obvious?" Allan asked. "You've found the killer."

Millicent cocked her gun. "Inside. Now."

Eve frowned. "Wait. You can't be serious. You don't fit the criteria."

"The what?"

"I mean, look at you. You sway with the slightest breeze. You're pint sized. You have large, doe-like eyes. Lana Bishop on the other hand—"

Allan moaned. "Eve, please don't make this worse."

"You don't seriously think she's going to shoot. What are you waiting for? I'll distract her while you grab the gun."

Millicent laughed.

"I said it out loud to give you the chance to come to your senses. And please stop pointing that gun at me. If you fire, everyone around here will hear."

Millicent took care of that. In the blink of an eye, she reached inside her bag and produced a silencer.

Chapter Fourteen

"WHATEVER YOU THINK you can get away with... you won't. Trust me, I speak from experience."

Millicent waved her gun. "Sit down and shut up."

For once, Eve did as told. After all, Millicent had a gun with a silencer. Unlike Eve, she'd come prepared.

"Okay, you have my attention," Eve said.

"You're still talking."

"Because you aren't." Eve folded her arms. "Go on, you have the floor. I'm listening."

Millicent moved over to the window and gazed out.

"Are we waiting for someone else?" She didn't get a response. Eve looked over at Allan. He sat opposite her, his hands clasped together, his jaw muscles twitching. She still couldn't understand why he hadn't taken her cue and lunged for the gun. At least he sat opposite her and not next to her. They still had a chance. If only she knew he'd co-operate and help her distract Millicent before the person she was waiting for arrived.

"So... here we are. Any chance you'll tell us why we're here? I mean, I know why I'm here. I'd organized to meet Lana Bishop. I guess she changed her mind about coming and sent you instead." Lana Bishop. She'd had her suspicions about her, but this confirmed it. More or less. "And now you're planning to do something really nasty to us. Before you do anything, it would be good to know why you killed Jon O'Brian."

Millicent chortled.

The last time she'd said something along those lines, the person holding the gun hadn't had any idea what she'd been referring to because she'd been an innocent bystander caught up in the middle of a sordid affair.

"Jon was superfluous."

"He outlived his usefulness?"

Millicent shrugged.

Eve was disappointed in her. In her place, she would have stuck to her guns and kept her mouth shut. Instead, Millicent wanted to boast. She'd bet anything it had all been her plan, her doing.

Eve decided to see what else she could get her to admit. "Lana played him."

"I lined her ducks in a row. I set her up with him."

"So, you're the mastermind matchmaker. I would never have guessed. In fact, I didn't. You had me fooled.

And everyone else. I bet the police didn't even bother to question you."

"That's right, you've been snooping around, sticking your nose where it doesn't belong."

Eve gestured with her hands. "Why does everyone say that about me?"

"Probably because it's true." Millicent laughed. "I'm going to do you a favor and put you out of your misery. If I don't, you're going to turn into the town busybody. So you can thank me now."

"Busybody? To tell you the truth, I don't go looking for trouble. It sort of finds me. I'm like a magnet and I'm starting to think there's a reason for that."

"Really?"

"Yes. Think of me as the gunslinger with the white hat. I'm one of the good guys and we all know the good guy always wins in the end."

"That sounds like fiction to me. How about I give you a taste of reality." Millicent pointed the gun at her, took a couple of steps and pressed it against her nose. "This is where I'm going to aim."

A scream swirled all the way up to her throat and got stuck there. Her one and only weapon and she hadn't been able to use it.

Millicent grinned and stepped away, her gaze sliding over to the window again.

Eve tried to draw moisture into her mouth, only then realizing it had dried up. If she caved in to fear now, her body would go into lockdown and she'd end up cowering.

Eve Lloyd, you are not a victim.

You're much stronger than this.

Focus.

She looked around her. Her gaze landed on a vase sitting on a table within reach. She tried to estimate its value. If she could rely on Allan to create a distraction, she might just be able to grab the vase and swing it at Millicent. Allan's chair was close to the fireplace. He could lunge for the fire poker...

She tried to communicate this idea with her eyes, but Allan wasn't even blinking.

"Allan."

He cleared his throat.

"Allan, I've been meaning to ask you. I saw you with Elizabeth-May a few days ago at Shelby's Table." When she saw him respond with a blink, she continued, "You appeared to be talking about having to go back to the Stevenson house and how no amount of money was worth it. What was she talking about?"

Again, he cleared his throat and appeared to be thinking about it.

"Come on," she coaxed him. "You can tell me."

He gave Millicent a furtive glance. "Charlotte was letting us in on an investment with huge returns," he murmured.

"Was this via Jon O'Brian?"

He nodded.

"Bummer. I guess you missed out."

He shook his head. "She'd already signed the deal. It's going ahead. New building with eighty percent occupancy before it's even been built."

"Wow." Eve saw Millicent check her watch and bite her bottom lip. She looked impatient. "Did she make it a condition to you attending the wedding?" She wouldn't be surprised if Charlotte had used bribery to force her so-called friends to come.

Allan shifted in his chair and gave a small nod. "Coming here was a detour for us."

A detour from the regular dazzling ports they no doubt visited. "This is the part I don't understand. Why here?"

"Ask her."

Eve thought he meant she should ask Charlotte but he actually looked up at Millicent.

Eve lowered her voice in a mock whisper, "Let me guess. Lana and Millicent twisted Jon's arm and forced him to hold the event here." They must have had something on him. Eve's mouth gaped open. "Did Lana threaten to tell Charlotte they'd been engaged?"

Allan's eyes widened. He hadn't known. But Millicent had. She gave a schoolgirl like snicker.

"Wow. They blackmailed Jon O'Brian and then Millicent killed him." She waited to hear her deny it. "It doesn't make sense. I thought he'd become Lana's go to person for contacts."

"The best laid plans of mice and men often go awry," Millicent murmured.

"What happened? Did Jon renege on the deal?"

"He could give orders but when the tables turned," Millicent shrugged. "He forced our hands. He said he'd already done enough, but we knew that after he married Charlotte he'd have access to even more people with serious money and bottomless budgets for parties."

"And that's when you fed him poisoned sushi." Eve hummed. "Fugu is not readily available—"

"It is if you know where to look. There's a black-market for it and some strange people out there wanting to get a taste of death."

"So, Jon dumped Lana and she agreed to keep silent so long as Jon hooked her up with wealthy clients. That sounds like a profitable setup."

"Even better now that we got rid of the middleman. He was taking a huge cut."

She'd been right about skimming... "And you think Charlotte is going to continue to do business with you and even recommend you to her friends. Will that include Dante? Are you expecting him to open doors for you?"

Millicent looked surprised.

"I saw him and Lana earlier today. I'm thinking

Dante requires a hefty entrance fee for those doors you want opened."

"You are a smart cookie. That's actually when Lana decided she couldn't risk having you around to ruin it for us."

"I wonder if Dante realizes he might be next? You probably already have a plan in the back-burner. Not poison because you wouldn't want to raise suspicion. Something else... a boating accident perhaps? One drink too many and he goes overboard, but only after you've set yourselves up with new contacts and accounts. Where does it stop, Millicent?"

"It stops with you shutting up."

"I can't help being chatty, especially as these might be my last words. As I told someone else before, you don't want to leave me guessing because I might come back and haunt you."

Millicent rolled her eyes. At least she didn't question her sanity the way the other person had...

Eve turned to Allen. "I bet you're kicking yourself for coming at all." She sat back and made a show of twiddling her thumbs. "Hey, Millicent. I think you've been stood up." She fixed her gaze on Allan who appeared to be more alert now. His eyes jumped around the room. She hoped that meant he was trying to think of a way out of their dilemma.

Eve stretched and yawned. "You can't kill us here, Millicent."

"Why not?" The lightness in Millicent's voice suggested she'd relaxed into her role. She felt confident. In charge. Empowered.

Eve imagined her thinking everything was working according to plan. Even better, she thought she'd get away with killing two innocent people. Eve could only hope she wasn't jumping at the bit and eager to get the job done.

"Why not? Because it'll give my inn a bad reputation. There's already been one death here. Another one will put us on the map for entirely the wrong reasons. It'll become the ideal destination for killers."

"What do you care?" Millicent chortled. "You'll be dead."

"That's beside the point."

"You're crazy."

Eve gave her a lifted eyebrow look that questioned her sanity. "Me? Crazy? I think you're projecting. For starters, you're the one with a gun and delusional enough to think you can poison one man and shoot a couple of other innocent people. Are you thinking of turning this into your next career? Surely you can see there's limited scope for advancement." Time, she needed to buy more time so Jack could get here and rescue her. But what if Lana got here first? That would be the end of her...

"You do love the sound of your own voice," Millicent said.

"Hey, someone has to be the voice of reason. It might as well be me. And here's something else I just thought about. You won't have to worry about criminal career progression because the place where you're going—"

Millicent pressed the gun against her nose again.

"You were saying?"

Her heart gave a protesting thump against her chest. "There's another reason why you can't kill us. Your DNA is everywhere. I bet you've lost track of what you've touched and every time you flick your hair, you're scattering more evidence. You'll never get away with it."

"I will if I torch the place after I put a bullet hole in you."

She hadn't thought of that. Her beautiful inn, reduced to ashes even before she'd had a chance to welcome her first guests. She should have purchased that expensive French oven. At least she would have had a moment of pleasure to think about while she drew her last breath...

Millicent waved the gun at her. "You didn't think of that." She laughed. "A nice fire will get rid of everything."

"Well, if you're going to do it... then go ahead. Shoot me."

"Eve."

She turned to Allan and watched a drop of perspiration trail down from his forehead. "What?"

"Please," he mouthed.

"Allan, I don't understand what you're so afraid of. There are two of us and only one of her. Okay, I'll give her an extra half point because she's holding a gun, but we still outnumber her."

Millicent dug inside her pocket and drew out a cell phone. She must have set it on vibrate because Eve didn't hear it ring.

"Hello. Where are you?"

She watched Millicent's eyebrows draw down. Something had happened. Plans had been changed and Millicent didn't look pleased about it.

"What do you mean?"

Her cheeks turned a violent shade of red.

"That's not what we agreed on."

Things were looking up, Eve thought. She had another quick glance around her. If she grabbed hold of the vase it could either land on Millicent's head or it could distract her long enough for Eve to lunge at her. In which case, Eve needed a backup plan. What else could she use as a weapon?

Her adrenaline? If she acted quickly, she could bend at the waist and ram into Millicent. Throw in a loud growl, anything to create chaos, and it might just work.

Speed. If she took action, she needed to be fast.

And, with any luck, Allan might snap out of his stupor and help her.

Millicent's voice hitched up. "We had it all worked out. Why are you changing the plans now?"

Eve frowned. Had she heard a car pulling up? Her heart punched against her chest again, the rhythm faster, more erratic.

Stay calm, Eve.

Millicent gave a throaty growl and disconnected the call.

"You know that call is going to be traced."

"You think I'd be stupid enough to use my own phone?" Millicent spat out.

When Allan shifted in his seat Millicent swung toward him.

"Don't move."

Okay. She was losing it. Panicking. Any minute now and she'd do something stupid...

Like shoot them.

La Cornue Château Series, Eve. Think of your beautiful French oven.

Yes. She didn't know how she'd pull it off, but she would buy it for her inn. And she would get it in aquamarine. Everything else in the kitchen would be eggshell white.

"You've been ditched," she taunted.

"Shut up."

"Lana's dumped you. Wake up, Millicent. You're

the sacrificial lamb. If you go ahead and shoot us, who's to say Lana won't be waiting for you outside ready to put a bullet in you. Someone has to take the fall." Eve forced herself to keep her eyes on Millicent but a part of her wanted desperately to look out the window and see who'd arrived. She was sure she'd heard a car pull up while Millicent had been on the phone with her accomplice. "Millicent, you know the police are never going to stop looking for the killer. And you're out of luck because the detective in charge is my boyfriend. He'll never rest until you're behind bars."

Millicent's eyes widened slightly. Her lips parted. Her gaze dropped.

Had Eve's warnings filtered through?

"You don't know what you're talking about." Millicent's voice carried an edge of doubt.

Eve scrambled to think of something else to add, something that would chip away at Millicent's determination.

"She's gone and left you to clean up the mess. But you're not walking away. You're in too deep. Someone can place you at the cocktail party. Trust me when I say Detective Jack Bradford is thorough. He'll never give up."

Millicent's eyes narrowed. Her lips firmed. She raised the gun and pointed it at Eve.

"What on earth is going on here?"

They all turned toward the hallway.

"Oh... oh... what... you're holding a..." Charlotte wavered, her eyes wide with shock and then Eve saw it.

That precise moment when Charlotte decided to take matters into her own hands.

Eve didn't know which came first.

The gunshot.

Or the large handbag being flung toward Millicent.

Then came the rage.

Charlotte exploded with an eruption that sent chills up Eve's spine.

"You shot my Birkin bag. Do you have any idea how long I had to wait to get that bag?" She rushed at Millicent.

Eve had a second to react, grabbing the vase, she threw it at Millicent's hand knocking the gun away just as Charlotte grabbed hold of Millicent's hair and began pulling, all the while continuing to rage about her Birkin bag.

Eve tackled them to the ground. She held Millicent down and made a mental note to ask Jill about Birkin bags.

"Charlotte. That's enough. We've got her pinned down."

Charlotte looked up, her perfect hair cascading around her shoulders. Her eyes narrowed down to slits.

"Charlotte. I never thought I'd say this. I'm so glad to see you."

Chapter Fifteen

"A *BIRKIN* BAG," Jill said in awe. "Handmade in France by Hermès. They're the same people who made the Grace Kelly bag. They're not sold to just anyone. If you're not a footballer's wife, super rich or royalty, you have to go on a waiting list."

"How much are we talking about? Several thousand dollars?" Eve asked.

"Five figures. It's all about exclusivity."

Eve threw another log in the fire and settled back on the couch.

"So, Charlotte saved the day," Jill mused.

Eve stared into space. She owed Charlotte her life. "Yes. She's the heroine." If she hadn't changed her mind about not wanting to talk to her...

Eve didn't want to think about it.

"Wow. And her handbag has a bullet hole in it now."

"Apparently the insurance refuses to pay. I wouldn't want to be in their shoes. They're going to get an earful from her."

Mira looked up from her book. "You have to admit, Eve, Charlotte has acquired some redeeming qualities. She could just as easily have run for her life, but instead, she rescued you."

"It doesn't make me indebted to her. Please, don't even suggest it."

"By the sounds of it, Millicent is the one who should be grateful," Mira said, " If you hadn't pulled Charlotte off her, she would have been torn to pieces."

"I think I heard Charlotte say she was suing her for criminal damages against her handbag." Eve closed her eyes and listened to the gentle crackle of the fire.

Jill sighed. "I was looking forward to the wedding. Any chance you and Jack might hurry it along and get married?"

"Not any time soon. Sorry."

"And the yachts. I liked going to those parties and meeting new people. I guess everyone's already left."

Eve nodded. "There was a mass exodus of yachts. We have the island to ourselves again." She checked her watch. Jack had promised to stop by after he got through all the paperwork. He'd arrived a few seconds after she'd thrown the vase at Millicent, his stern expression speaking volumes. She'd have a lot of explaining to do...

She considered calling him when she saw him wave at her from the back door.

"Jack. Come in. That must have been quick work. I didn't expect you to come by until tomorrow or the next day. Does this mean you've already caught Lana Bishop?"

He nodded. "We found her aboard Dante Hildegard's yacht."

"Her alibi. What made you think to look for her there?"

He gave her a small smile. "You gave us the lead. You saw her with Dante and then she didn't turn up at the house. We figured she would have tried to position herself somewhere with an alibi. Fortunately for us, she still hadn't disposed of her cell phone so we were able to match the call she made to Millicent's cell phone."

"If Millicent hadn't told me she'd sourced the Fugu from the black-market, I would have pointed the finger at Dante. He's recently been to Japan."

"We already have two people in custody. I think that's enough for now."

"Have you figured out which one did the deed?"

"A team effort. Millicent sourced the Fugu liver, Lana prepared the *pâté*, and Millicent took it to the party, hanging around long enough to make sure it was used."

"But who thought of it all?"

"They bounced ideas off each other, much the same

way you do with Jill. Eventually they reached the same conclusion. They had to get rid of Jon O'Brian. By the way, Charlotte McLain gave us a piece of her mind saying if you hadn't cornered the suspects we'd still be chasing our tails."

"Sorry. She can be hard."

He brushed his hand across her cheek. From the first moment she'd met Jack, she'd known his concern for her was genuine. "Is that chocolate I smell?"

"Yes. My chocolate fudge tart is just about ready to come out of the oven. I made one earlier in the week but Jill says she didn't get enough and after what I put her through, she claims I owe her. You'll have to wait for it to cool down. Come on in. We're in the sitting room sharing war stories."

"Hang on."

"Oh, boy. Here it comes."

"Eve."

"Yes?"

"Do you realize how close you came this time?"

"I thought you appreciated my input."

"I do, but in future—"

"Oh, no. This is it. We've had enough murder and mayhem on the island. Chances are we're now in the clear."

"In future," he repeated, "Would you mind sticking to suspect lists and theory?"

"No more field work?"

"No more rogue tactics."

"But I let you know exactly what I was doing. I kept you right in the loop."

"You set up a meeting with your top suspects and then you ditched Jill to go it alone."

"It goes to show how responsible I am." She sighed. "Look, you have nothing to worry about. I'm going to be so busy setting up my inn, I won't have any time to get mixed up in any more murders."

"Promise?"

"Absolutely. You have my word."

Made in United States
North Haven, CT
17 October 2022